An Time

To Ellie,

One of the few Brits I can stand. Thank you for becoming my friend

- Theodore K. Monroe

AAWT:
An Adventure With Time
Theodore K. Monroe

Book Cover by Theodore. K. Monroe

First edition 2023

979-8-223-50198-5

Dedications.

This book is dedicated to a multitude of people as I'm not sure I'll ever get the chance to do this again. I won't be mentioning many names, for the sake of anonymity.

Firstly, thank you to my beautiful mother who raised me alone, and helped nurture the creativity and imagination I've had since I was a child. Words could never be enough. Dankie ma, ek lief jou lots and lots like jelly tots.

Thank you to Hessey and his mother, who both suffered through endless amounts of me bending their ears, telling them about every story or thought that ever crossed my mind all throughout highschool.

The same thanks goes out to anyone else who I've ever bored stiff and who never told me to shut up, no matter how badly they wanted me to.

Thanks to my big brother Te, a man after my own heart. I love you bro.

Here's to the smokers and non-smokers who met nearly every night at the picnic table, and to The Penguin. I love you all, and I hope you're all well.

In the same crowd are all the friends I've ever had. Don't be afraid to reach out, I've been thinking of you all, I'm just not so good at reaching out.

日本でできた友達全員に感謝しています。あなたのような人は他にいません。あなたは私の人生を、生きる価値のあるものにしてくれました。

船橋でできた友達、そして秋葉原の家族へ、愛を込めて。

(Thank you Yukina-san for translating this for me!)

And thank you to all the girls I've loved and lost.

You helped me write heartbreak, but I hope you're all well.

And thank *you*.

Be careful!

Chapter One
"A day in the life of me."

Time paused again.

I cursed under my breath and kicked a loose stone which had been minding its own business, sitting between the cracks of the pavement, and it was sent skittering across the sidewalk and onto the road. With a scowl on my face I shook my fist at the early morning sun which sat perfectly still in its trajectory across the bay; its journey temporarily halted. It wasn't the sun's fault, but I felt I had to blame something.

For how long I waited I couldn't be sure as the hands on my watch never moved, and never would, and I was left to find my own entertainment in a still world. When time decided to kick itself back into gear Nina took a few seconds to realize I was no longer by her side, and when she did her sentence half-spoken halted, as did her pace, and she turned to see me sitting atop a cobblestone wall. It served as a barrier protecting pedestrians from a very long drop onto the roof of houses that sat below, and I perched precariously balanced between safety and certain death, trying to get comfortable.

A knowing smile pushed at Nina's cheeks as she looked up at me.

"It happened again, didn't it?" she asked, despite already having the answer. I swung my legs over and dropped off the wall, receiving some nasty groundshock which ricocheted up my right leg as I landed, and with a wince I gave her a nod. In response she clapped her hands together rapidly and a little noise of excitement escaped her. I sighed.

If I could have somehow given Nina the burden of my ability, I would've. She seemed to find far more enjoyment in it than I ever could. Ever since I discovered I could pause time and had revealed it to her the year before she'd spent countless nights awake coming up with theories and experiments for me to participate in. Most of which led to no new discoveries other than some stuff she'd figured out about momentum or some such, I never really listened. There wasn't much she could do without being Unpaused and I had eventually grown tired of conducting her experiments, so after the initial excitement had died down I would never have Paused again. But it wasn't long after that time would stop of its own accord, something that Nina found very interesting indeed. And something that made daily life a living hell for me.

I knew that soon to come would be her usual query and that whatever I answered would be hastily scribbled in a notebook she had specifically for the Pauses. One with a bright red cover, inside of which sat decorated titles above pages of documented data she'd highlighted and color-coded. Little diagrams cutely scribbled in the margins helped to visualize the theories she'd jotted down in her flowy handwriting.

She checked the time on my watch and wrote it down.

"How long was the pause?" she asked, her pen moving before I'd even opened my mouth to answer. I tugged on the edge of her sleeve and urged her to continue the walk to school as she questioned me, and she followed along without even looking up.

"Too long."

"Did you activate the Pause?"

I pulled her to the side so she wouldn't walk into a lamppost and she dutifully stepped behind me.

"No."

That word came out far too naturally at this point, eager and awaiting to answer that specific question. The amount of scribbling I heard was always disproportionate to the amount of words I'd said, and despite myself I felt a little curious as to what she'd written down. Shoving my hands in my pocket I tried to play it cool and looked away.

"What did you do during the pause?"

"Stretched. Looked at the ocean. Sat on the wall."

She nodded.

"Did you see anything out of the ordinary?" Came the final question.

I shook my head. Sometimes I considered lying just to give Nina something to write about. Make up a story about seeing a bird flying, or hearing a cricket sing, or maybe even allude to there being another person walking around. But nothing interesting ever *did* happen, and I didn't exactly want to lie about it. Truth be told, I felt a little guilty for not using my power but it's not like I ever wanted it in the first place. I was a regular guy in a regular world, and I wanted to keep it that way. Watching television and sleeping in class was more than enough excitement for me. It was more trouble than it was worth anyway, because when time paused at random –as it tended to do- it was usually with rather inconvenient timing. Imagine trying to have a shower when all the water stops midair, and you're left cold and naked and covered in soap. Or imagine the sheer impatience you'd feel if the mailman was just about to hand you your favourite monthly magazine, and now all you could do was stand there waiting so he doesn't see you disappear into thin air.

That would only bring more trouble to the relative peace I had.

"You two like making me wait... don't you?" Asked a deep and sultry voice from ahead, interrupting our conversation. It originated from the beanpole leaning against the streetlight ahead of us with his lips pursed. Half-frame spectacles sat loosely halfway down the bridge of his nose, gloriously reflecting the morning sun as did the shock of his blonde hair. Standing straight up as it was, it appeared like a golden halo.

The odd pose and demeanor would have given this stranger an air of erotic intrigue and mystery, had he actually been a stranger. Tobetobii -better known as 'Tobey'- was trying to seduce either Nina or I. It was one of his running gags... at least, I *hope* it was a gag.

"Come on man, cover yourself up!" I protested, shielding my eyes from the sight of his toned stomach peering through the curtains of his unbuttoned shirt. He looked down at his stomach, then with an innocent eyebrow raised he peered over the rim of his glasses.

"Who, me?"

Yes you!

Nina put her notebook into her bag as she laughed. "You don't want to get arrested for indecent exposure again do you, Tobey?"

Tobey cleared his throat and began re-buttoning his shirt, his voice back to its usual cadence and higher octave. "I'm sure you remember that it was an honest misunderstanding, and that all charges were dropped," he meekly protested.

"I seriously can't believe you got away with that stunt," I sighed, trying my hardest to wipe the memory from my brain, and successfully doing so. I was very good at not thinking.

Tobey joined us for the remainder of the walk as was our usual morning routine, telling us all about the crazy night he'd had before. Whether he was complaining about the new law affecting a foreign country's durian exportation, or recounting a battle he'd had in a chess tournament, he was always fun to listen to. Even if I could never tell if he was lying or just *really* embellishing his tales.

The road up to our highschool was a grueling hike for the entire student body as the schmuck who decided to build it years ago had placed it atop a cliff, and the only roads that led to it were winding and steep; rising and falling with the peaks of the surrounding hills. The town was also so small it didn't have any bus routes, so if you didn't have a vehicle the only thing you could do was trek up. I suppose maybe the architect or designer (or whoever built it) thought that having a learning institution built on the highest hill in town would be a sign of dignity. But now I'm just making things up. I have no idea what was going through his mind when he made this particular decision. Although if that had been his line of thinking he'd have been beat, as the North Academy *-the* private school- had been built on an even higher cliff-face.

Huh. Maybe it *was* a sign of dignity.

The closer we got to the school the more of our fellow students appeared, each carrying a varying degree of enthusiasm for the day of learning ahead. The sky was a rich blue liquid aquamarine and soft cotton-candy clouds floated miles and miles above, blissfully unaware companions to seagulls squawking overhead. The abhorrent heat and sticky humidity that usually came hand in hand with the middle-of-summer-cicadas hadn't set in, and for that I was thankful. It meant I could enjoy the morning commute without arriving at school drenched in sweat.

"Who decided that 0.5 rounded up anyway?" Tobey groaned, retelling how he was 'cheated' out of a few coins of change. "Math is just numbers made up by humans, who gets to decide what means what? Who could possibly be granted the power to negate the rounding-uppage of 0.6?"

"I wonder how different the world would be if the decimal point to round up was 0.1 higher," Nina pondered, head tilted. "Our understanding of mathematical fundamentals would be different, but that doesn't even take into account the effects it would have on civilization."

"The limitations and rules set by a few 'intellectuals' create nothing but a safe little box to think within. That's not how the universe works." Tobey's passionate rant was reaching levels of distaste for the higher echelon of education that my mind could never possibly hope to understand. I knew that two plus two equaled four, but Tobey was adamant that that wasn't always the case and that my human brain was far too limited to understand the true mathematics of the universe.

"Enough with the nerdy crap!" I shouted, throwing my hands into the air. My brain was already hurting and we weren't even at school yet. "Have your mathematical philosophy discussion later, I'm trying to enjoy the sun and I don't need you two harping on about numbers!"

Tobey placed a hand on his chest. "Don't yuck my yums, man."

"Screw your yums! My brain is perfectly fine!"

He muttered something under his breath that I couldn't hear, but that made Nina giggle. She struggled for air and clutched at her stomach.

"Hey!"

Nina giggled even louder, but Tobey punched my arm.

"You're in a good mood," he said.

"You sure ain't helpin'!"

The school bells rang as we approached the school grounds although the incessant ringing did nothing to inspire anybody to walk any faster. Students discussed what they'd watched on TV the previous night as they were funneled through a main gate and led beneath two absolutely giant oak trees. The grounds at the front of the school where they stood were covered in a haze of fiery orange leaves, prematurely shed in their eager anticipation for autumn. The sheer amount of leaves was staggering, and rather problematic as they had been sneaking into the main building through open windows and taking refuge from the summer heat between the books of your open backpack.

The embers of the oaks fell gracefully and spun around Nina's head in a silent dance. Past the towering oaks and into the main building, we stopped by the shoe lockers now crowded with hundreds of students. This part of the day was always a mad scramble spent wrestling your fellow classmates out of the way so you weren't late to class.

"Hey Nina, are you gonna be on the roof this break?" I called out so she could hear me over the commotion. I listened intently for her answer as I unlocked my cubby and retrieved my shoes.

"Yeah, I'll be there. I don't have anything else going on. Besides, I see you didn't bring any lunch... again." She replied from the far end of the row, peering over her cubby door.

I hadn't even realized I'd forgotten my bag at home.

What would I do without her?

"Awesome," I said. More to myself than anyone else.

"Not gonna ask me?" Tobey complained from the room. How he heard me I could only imagine. The supersonic hearing or something. I slipped my school sh stood straight, stretching to see him and locking eyes in the pr

"Nope! You don't give me free food!"

"I do. You just don't eat it!" he protested.

"Try not burning it!" I countered and he scoffed, rolling his eyes.

"I burn it on purpose. It adds texture."

"That doesn't make it edible!"

Nina waved goodbye to Tobey and I as most of her schedule was different to ours, although by some stroke of luck Tobey shared every class with me. Whether that stroke of luck was good or bad I was still unsure.

We made our way to Homeroom jostled around by the hundreds of students flooding the hallways, but we managed to make it to our seats just as the bell rang; Tobey's at the front of the class directly opposite the teacher, whereas I sat near the back where I could remain undetected as I napped. Mr. Washy –our bumbling and unfortunate-looking teacher– walked into the classroom and we all stood and bowed before I reclined and got comfy, spending the next hour pretending to study.

I don't think Mr. Washy's fishbowl spectacles allowed him to see me slacking off at such a distance, or he possibly just didn't care. I was usually daydreaming about sitting on a beach with Miss. Morina Winslow. In stark contrast, Tobey spent most of the time nose-deep in three inch thick textbooks which he had stacked rather precariously atop his desk. The majority of them were completely unrelated to whatever topic was being taught, however he always seemed to possess as much knowledge as the teachers on whatever subject they taught.

sometimes more. That was Tobey though; endlessly knowledgeable on the most irrelevant information.

The bell signifying the end of Homeroom rang, interrupting the infomercials I had memorized and let play on a loop in my head. I shoved a notebook into my desk and automatically my feet began the march to the rooftop garden where I met Nina every day during the breaks. Tobey found himself by my side most days, but it was not uncommon that he would be absent, performing tasks and quests of a dizzying variety for an entire cast of characters who I had never met.

Some days I liked to take the scenic route, walking through each hallway of each floor, looking out the windows that faced the bay and reading the posters for events I would never attend and clubs I would never join. I tended to avoid the music rooms though.

Whenever Nina was busy doing something for someone –which was more often than I'd like– Tobey and I usually meandered on our walk to fill the time. Nina was far too eager to help out anyone who asked, no matter what it was. She'd even become an honorary School Council member, owing to the amount of help she'd given them. Today was a lucky break though so we opted to skip the garden, gym, and track sections of our walk in favor of getting to the roof faster, and in turn the sandwich she had waiting for me. We made our way up using the stairwell because Tobey didn't want to risk getting in trouble for climbing the fire escape, even though I thought it had some of the best views on campus. No matter how much I tried to convince him we wouldn't get caught he never relented, but I didn't really mind anyway.

I swung the dark green door that led to the rooftop open, and as we stepped through Nina waved at us from a picnic blanket she'd laid down near a park bench.

Would it technically be called a roof bench?

In any case, a long time ago she'd found me on the roof lying on my back and watching the clouds. She'd sighed deeply but lay next to me and pointed out a cloud that looked like a jack rabbit. I argued it looked more like a walrus. We started meeting on the roof more and more and the collection of house plants she'd accrued from somewhere grew, which meant that my fortress of solitude had become her garden over the space of a year. But I didn't mind. The plants were good company. Ever since then it had become a sort of ritual for us to lie among the plants and cloud-watch. Or maybe it was closer to a tradition. Or maybe it was neither, and was simply something we did together.

The three of us lay on our backs watching the clouds amble across the sky whilst listening to the sounds of the school. The enthusiastic chatter of a clique of girls exchanging gossip, or the angry yell of someone challenging how legitimate the goal kick was. Even the hushed whisper of a confession and the befuddled recipient looking for the word 'yes' found its way up here. There was something I enjoyed about the soundscape of the school, even if I couldn't get along with the people providing it. It wasn't them, not really. It was me. There was something I couldn't quite grasp about people.

"What crime would be bad enough for you to turn me in?" Nina asked out of the blue. Her gaze was still fixed on the sky.

"You mean like, theft?" I asked.

"You'd turn me in for theft?"

"No. Well... it depends on what you stole. Is it an object like a car or something closer to organ theft or tax evasion?"

Tobey sat up then, and with a face as cold as steel declared: "I will be cold and dead before I report someone for tax evasion! Don't worry Nina, your secret is safe with me."

She slapped the top of his head. "I haven't stolen anything! I'm just asking!"

Tobey muttered as he lay back down. "I just said I'd cover for you and now you're assaulting me... you're gonna be a terrible criminal one day."

She looked at me and rolled her eyes. "Would you report me if I turned Tobey into compost for my plants?"

I shrugged. "Be my guest."

Tobey sat up again, this time with his eyebrows raised at a ridiculously dramatic angle. "Shoot, I forgot I have a private lesson with Nurse Singer!" he shouted and leapt to his feet, clutching his half-eaten sandwich tightly in his fist as he rushed to the door. He got halfway across the roof before stopping to peer back over his shoulder with a weak smile. "She's giving me a lesson on... 'human anatomy' you see..."

What a lame excuse.

"I think you made him wet himself," I laughed, lying back down after he'd disappeared.

"Am I that scary?" Nina asked, giving a cursory glance around the rooftop, making sure no one was within earshot so she could finally ask what had been on her mind all morning. I could tell just how badly she'd wanted to ask by how quickly the words came tumbling out of her mouth.

"Do you think that maybe other people are causing the Pauses?"

I rolled onto my side to look at her.

"I've been thinking... Maybe the reason Pauses happen so randomly for you is because other people can control time too, and you're... for lack of a better term, 'immune,' to their time pause."

"But I've never seen anyone else move when time's paused," I countered, taking another bite of Nina's sandwich. Today she'd made a pan-fried chicken and lettuce sandwich which had been filled with some kind of homemade sauce I would kill to get the recipe for. The chicken was still juicy, and had been lightly crumbed so there was a slight crunchiness to the sandwich which added a satisfying feeling in your mouth when you bit down. The sauce was tangy, yet sweet, and complimented the meal without making the bread soggy. I think cooking was Nina's special talent.

Yeah, okay, she *was* the fastest runner in the school (only because I was out of commission!), but her culinary skills were from another planet. She could be a chef, or even a sous-chef!

"It's not exactly like you've ever bothered to look." She rolled her eyes.

True.

"Although maybe they're not around here," she continued after a moment.

So you're saying some bozo on the other side of the planet could be the one pausing time, and I'm just a victim to his will? Great...

Nina slipped the red journal out of her bag and flipped open to a diagram with dots and lines, none of which I understood, and pointed at specific nodes on the chart.

"I've been examining the data, and I've noticed that for the majority of the time Pauses tend to occur outside of school or work hours, both before and after. With a few exceptions. However, there doesn't seem to be a *definite* pattern. They truly *are* occurring randomly. If it was the universe's doing I'm sure there would be some pattern I could follow. My hypothesis is that you're not the only one who can pause time."

As much as I brushed the idea off I thought that perhaps she was right. I mean, just because I hadn't seen anyone else didn't mean there weren't others like me out in the world pausing time for their own gain. Although what was the likelihood of one person being able to pause time, let alone two?

My original plan had been to use Study Hall as a free one hour nap session, but one fateful day long ago I had been bestowed the social obligation of joining David and Eileen's clique after having taken the last seat available in the library. Which just so happened to be at their table. Study Hall didn't have a structured seating arrangement which meant that I was free to sit somewhere else, but it also meant that no matter how hard I tried to evade them they'd find my hiding spot and drag their seats over to join me. Over time I had learned that it was far easier to admit defeat and join them, and over time I found myself enjoying their company too.

David and Eileen were complete opposites of one another. David was a ball-throwing, bat-hitting, kick-and-tackle kind of guy who always managed to show up to class covered in bruises or dirt, even if it was the first period of the day. Eileen, however, was far more concerned with burning through whatever reading materials she could get her hands on. Her favourite topic being the infamously boring Inter-Gellic Bohmian Transfer. She and Tobey had that in common. While our varied interests differed vastly and we didn't really hang out together outside of Study Hall, we all got along together. Why they kept me around I don't know because they got along so well by themselves that it had even sparked rumours that they were long lost twins separated by birth... or were dating. Surprisingly enough neither rumour was true despite the fact that the both of them were painfully attractive and personable.

When David had forgiven me, I don't know, but it seemed that everything was all water under the bridge at this point. No apologies necessary. Unless he was only tolerating me for Eileen's sake which I wouldn't blame him for.

They were already deep in conversation by the time I'd arrived.

"Hey!" Eileen said as I'd sat down, her tone cheery and dreamy. "We were just talking about the teleporters. Have you heard?" She was deeply interested in the occult and urban legends, one of the few things she liked that weren't entirely bound within the pages of a book.

"Please... do tell..." huffed Tobey, covered in sweat after having arrived quite suddenly in a flurry of rushing footsteps. I gave him a raised eyebrow and he gave me a wink in return.

"Oh, Tobey!" Eileen exclaimed, eager for more ears in the audience. "Have you heard?"

"About the one Leopald saw off main street?"

"No." Eileen leaned in with a grin. "This is a new one."

I looked at Eileen and she nodded dramatically, her glasses slipping down her nose. David was beside her, sitting with his massively muscled arms crossed and his gaze locked on Eileen. He was probably as eager to hear about the teleporters as Tobey.

It seemed I had somehow surrounded myself with occultism fanatics. Only *I* could be so lucky.

"A bunch of my girlfriends were west of main in the old shopping district when they saw a guy turn a corner and disappear!"

"He didn't just go inside? Like, with a door or something?" I asked.

"No! I specifically asked that but they said there was nowhere he could have gone, not unless he leapt fifteen feet in the air and climbed through a window in the blink of an eye!"

Maybe you've got a talented gymnast on the loose. Scary.

Tobey 'hmmed' beside me, rubbing his chin in a wannabe facsimile of 'the thinker'. He probably thought he looked cooler than he did. "You said they saw a guy, right? Well, Leopald claims he saw a girl."

"So we have at least two teleporters in town..." David nodded thoughtfully.

"Ooh!" Eileen exclaimed, almost screaming in delight. "That might mean we have a bunch of Augurs in town!"

"Augurs, here?" I asked, dumbfounded. I hadn't considered that I might have been an Augur myself. But how and when would that have occured? I always imagined being Augmented came with bright flashing lights and some bewildering transformation.

"There was that City that exiled a bunch of them into the wasteland a few years back," Eileen chirped. Even though I wasn't fond of the conversation topic, I could listen to her talk all day.

"Weren't they mercenaries?" David tilted his head.

"The mercenary corps had Augurs in their ranks," Tobey clarified, his tone serious and clear. He'd make a good teacher. "The Augurs who resisted, and whoever stood with them, were exiled. Those who didn't resist were enlisted by the City."

"So what, a City is invading?" I mockingly gawked, hoping they'd see how ridiculous this idea they had was. "That happened on a totally different continent if you care to remember."

"Could be that the exiled ones are emigrating. Or maybe the City sent a spy." Tobey suggested with a shrug of his shoulders.

Impossible!

"They could be assassins!" Eileen gasped and I sighed. "That could explain all the mysterious slashings, they were marked men!"

Even more impossible!

"It's reported that nobody has even seen the slasher so that theory might fit." Tobey nodded in firm agreement.

"So we've uncovered that there are at least two teleporters. A boy and a girl. Okay, that clears up the confusion." Eileen grinned enthusiastically then turned to me. "What do you think?"

"I don't!" I laughed, and got shushed by the aged librarian. But as they spoke, coming up with theories and ideas, I was reminded of my own power. Maybe there was some merit to those stories.

"What would you do if you could teleport?" David asked.

"Oh you know me," Eileen said with a fist raised and a stoic expression. "I'd use my power to rule the world!"

When lunchtime finally rolled around Tobey said: 'I'll meet you on the roof later!' with a wave as he hurried to wherever his next destination lay. As per usual I had no idea what he was up to, or what destination he was rushing towards. I could only hope that he wasn't up to something nefarious. Although, knowing him, I wasn't too hopeful.

His departure meant I was alone for my usual walk, allowing me to enjoy it as much as I wanted, taking the long route. It started off nicely. I was in a good mood, the sky was clear, the air was warm, and nobody had bothered me. But as I came close to the little courtyard they'd built around a weeping willow I saw a vile 'being' through the yard's surrounding windows, and I immediately turned down a corridor to evade the threat. Unfortunately for me though I was destined to cross paths with Oscar Owens that day. Our destinies were bound to the other it seemed. He turned the corner at the far end of the hallway just as I rounded my own. Turning around now would only invite trouble so I soldiered on.

To put it simply, Oscar had the winning combination of being the offspring of a rich and powerful family, while only being somewhat psychopathic. His parents weren't even that bad but somehow they'd bred a monster. He was the bane of most students' existence and a menace to society in general. To me he was all that and more.

To display his power he'd stride through the middle of the halls and smirk as the student body gave him a wide berth, scurrying away to avoid bumping into him and facing his wrath. Today –as he did every day– he strolled comfortably with his back straight and hands shoved deeply in his pockets, along with a bored expression painted on his face. As he saw me I noticed the corner of his lip curl upwards all of a millimeter. It was such a minor change in expression that signified he'd gone from bored to bemused, but I had learned his facial expressions long ago. No one else but me would have noticed.

"It's a beautiful view, isn't it?" he asked. Rhetorically I assumed, as I had no idea what he was referring to, but he then nodded towards the window and the bright blue ocean beyond. "So many people, uncountable millions, have died before they ever got to see anything half as beautiful as that." He said this while nodding slightly, as if he were agreeing with himself. As he turned his gaze to me I almost physically faltered. My limbs felt encased in concrete.

Eyes as cold as ice stared at me through his unkempt black bangs, and I struggled to hold his gaze. "Every day we look at the ocean. Does it mean anything to us? No. Beauty is lost on us in abundance." He hung his head. "There is too much abundance, but you already know that. It all means nothing because we don't have to *give* anything to see it. We don't have to fight for it, struggle for it. Risk life and limb for it. Not like those who came before." He looked up at me, seemingly waiting for my response.

I didn't say anything.

It was easier to keep things simple with him, as he enjoyed twisting your words and finding meaning you never intended.

"Abundance negates meaning," he sighed as he stepped forward and placed a hand on my shoulder. Oscar seemed *tired*. "And the only thing with meaning is what you've lost. What you remember."

Was this his way of actually talking to me? No, impossible. He would never.

"Life isn't like the movies. Is it?"

I'd heard this before. I could quote it off by heart. Word for word.

"There is no happy ending. The curtains don't close and the credits don't roll, it just keeps going."

Just shut up.

His hand slipped from my shoulder and he marched on silently.

I waited for a few seconds before sighing in relief, heaving heavily and letting the tension fall from my shoulders before realizing just how lightheaded I was. My hands were shaking.

That was the tamest interaction I'd had with him for a long while, and for that I was more than grateful. Those days I gave his words no meaning as he was only a few beers and a decade or two away from becoming that weird old guy who speaks in riddles and sleeps in a park, previously incarcerated for eating a cat.

Too specific?

I threw a glance over my shoulder to make sure no one was watching before I clambered out the window and onto the fire escape outside. I had decided that after encountering Oscar, any enjoyment I could squeeze out of the rest of my walk wasn't worth it and that I should just go see Nina instead. I wanted to see Nina, badly. After closing the window and concealing my exit, I went up, climbing the metal steps and immediately recognizing the bickering voices I could hear one floor higher. I was not surprised in the least to see Lucy Lou and Akera Carter complaining about something or other, chatting in between puffs of a shared cigarette which I plucked out of Akera's mouth and placed in my own. She scowled upon my sudden appearance, her doll-like features crumpling in extreme annoyance.

Lucy was blonde as can be, and her skin was pale to match, but everything about Akera was perfectly average. Her almond shaped eyes, her pointed face, and her black hair would have been the perfect example of the average person in my country had it not been for the loud earrings and the scowl she always wore.

"Hey, we were just deciding on whether or not to ditch last period. Wanna come?" Lucy –the friendlier of the two– asked. It was odd really, how they'd turned out.

Or were still turning out, rather.

I'd heard from Nina that these two had been very focused on their education some time ago, however (for some reason I had never heard because it had been omitted from her retellings), Akera had seemingly become a delinquent overnight and had dragged her best friend down with her. Over just the course of a few months the two had gained quite a reputation for cussing teachers out and ditching class, and apparently the times they *had* attended they hadn't always been sober.

I exhaled the smoke and shook my head. "No thanks. I'd love to join in but I don't want my grades to suffer." Akera rolled her eyes and took the cigarette from me.

She knew I was as bad as them.

"I also doubt I could provide much insight concerning your discussion about '*this nation's hottest boy-bands*;'" I chuckled, and her scowl turned violent whilst Lucy laughed. I barely avoided an elbow directed towards my ribs as I scuttled away and carried on with my journey up two more floors. Climbing over the ladder I saw Nina and we waved at one another,

"Hey!" she called out as I swung over the railing, but my foot got stuck and I fell face-first into the ground with a scream.

Embarrassing.

Plus I got gravel in my mouth.

"Are you okay!?" I heard Nina yell. As I readied a reply I became aware that time had paused, so I groaned and got up, rubbing the stones off my face and forgoing the response. A Pause didn't have a particular feeling attached to it. There was no hair-raising sensation that travelled down my spine or a dramatic flash of power. It was merely something I just *knew.*

A flock of birds remained in flight just above the rooftop, in a cluster of chaotic wing flaps. My sudden appearance and subsequent fall must have spooked them. I limped over to where Nina was sitting and parked next to her on the picnic blanket as I admired the craftsmanship of their wings. Technology didn't work when time was paused which meant that television, or a mp3 player, or even my phone weren't options available to help pass the time. However, things I affected myself would keep moving so I could throw a ball at a wall and it would bounce back unless I dropped it and it eventually rolled to a stop. Nina had deduced that it had something to do with momentum.

While I wasn't the biggest fan of books I could peruse a magazine, but I didn't often have one on me when a Pause would occur, so most of the time all I could do was sit and wait. Occasionally my mind would wander and I'd think a little too hard. I'd look at the people going about their day, blissfully unaware that there were a few extra minutes or hours in their day that I had to endure. I'd seen hundreds of people locked in a moment of time that they'd soon forget, the countless smiles of friends laughing at a joke, and I'd seen the quiet expressions held by those walking alone. Businessmen often looked sombre. Tired of working I supposed. Or maybe even the woes of adult life.

I used to wander around town during the Pauses to see what was happening in the lives of my hometownspeople. One day I'd seen some kids who were playing with a dog at the park, giggling at the slobbery kisses it was giving them after returning a tennis ball. One of the kids looked particularly disgusted, holding his wet hand as far away as he could, and nearby on a park bench an old woman sat watching them play. She'd been quietly smiling to herself. At the far end of the park a girl my age was sitting beneath a tree crying, though it was hard to tell from afar. Her face had broken and tears hung in midair, but her hair covered her face so you couldn't tell unless you were right next to her. And there was no one but me. I'd sat by her side and placed a hand on her shoulder, but there was nothing else I could have done.

I did leave a letter for her, tucked away within her bag,

I wonder if she'd ever read it.

On another day work had just let out and so the streets were filled with hundreds of men in suits who had just finished their shift, or were just starting them. All looked weary and had loosened their ties so their necks could breathe. Kids and teenagers were clumped together in their friendship groups and mothers walked home with their children, hands full of shopping bags. Delinquents hung around in alleyways with cigarettes hanging limply in their mouths, almost always accompanied by a scowl. As I wandered the streets an unimaginable number of people surrounded me, each walking to their own destinations, their heads filled with their own thoughts, their own memories, their own opinions and relationships, their lives affecting each other in an expansive web of influence that stretched for miles and miles, completely invisible. I got lost in the crowd, and stopped wandering after that.

I shook the memory from my mind and looked at Nina instead. Her face was troubled and she looked as if she was about to call out to me again before time had stopped her. I had grown bored of watching the still clouds, and sighed at the uncaring world, so leaning on my hand I stared at her face instead. At her hazel eyes that were like a forest floor, and her top lip that always looked smudged. She had bags under her eyes that gave off the impression she was always on the cusp of either crying or falling asleep at any given second, but I liked that.

Reaching out I tousled her bangs, pushing them to one side and smiling at the wild hair sticking out the left side of her head.

Her bed hair.

She'd attempted to fight it but over the years her pillow had always remained the victor. Smiling to myself I traced my thumb over the freckle by her mouth. She was small when time was still, but when it ticked by she was the queen of the world.

The birds' wings flapped overhead and the cars on the road honked at one another. Nina's voice caught in her throat as her eyes settled on mine and her eyelashes fluttered for a moment.

"W... what are you doing?" she stuttered. I felt her face grow hot beneath my hand.

"Hold on, just a second," I mumbled, and Nina sat there as I played with her hair, sprucing it all up so it looked like she'd just clambered out of bed. After a moment or two I leaned back and admired my handiwork, nodding in approval. You had to admit that Nina looked good untidy.

She looked good all the time.

"You just messed up my hair."

"Well yeah, but it suits you."

"You like my hair like this?" she said in a voice so soft I had to lean in to hear her words, and it was a hair's breadth away from her face when I realized just how close I was, and what I had just been doing, and I immediately jerked back.

"Uh, yeah," I chuckled weakly, scratching the back of my head.

The silence was killing me.

"You smell like smoke."

"...Sorry."

A few minutes later the door to the roof burst open with such immense force that I wondered how it remained intact. Tobey rushed out, leaping over an airconditioning unit and coming to a stop with a skid. Through heavy breaths he looked up at us.

"Did you know that there's a new transfer student starting tomorrow?" he gasped, words coming out like a speeding train.

"No way, who? From where?" I asked, stunned by this new information.

"A foreigner..." he huffed, then looked at me with a sly smile. "And a girl at that!"

"Actually, I knew. I've been asked to look after her," Nina interjected, having finished putting away her red notebook. Then she pouted. "I already told you this!"

"Oh?" we said in unison, turning to her. "Where's she from?"

"I can't remember exactly... somewhere in the Europan Provinces though. I volunteered to be her 'designated friend,'" she said with a cheerful smile.

"Oh don't tell me..." I sighed, planting a hand on my forehead.

"Yep! I'll be showing her where her classes are, spending lunch with her, and helping her adjust to our culture!" She had a beaming grin on her face.

There goes my peace and quiet. Flying away like a startled pigeon.

"Wait..." I said, remembering the one thing I'd learned this whole year. "Aren't the Europan Provinces allied with the Northern Cities? I thought that we were at a stalemate with them?"

They both looked severely impressed with the factoid Eileen had drilled into my head through practicing her history speech and having me hold her cue cards. David had been absent that day, otherwise he would have done it.

"You're thinking of the Europan Isles, The Provinces banded together and became independent so they could form an alliance with the Lake Cities," Tobey clarified.

Way too much information for my brain to handle... or possibly care about.

Something wasn't adding up either. I had never once met a foreigner who hadn't sailed in from the docks to deliver mail or cargo, and certainly not one who was a student, so how could she possibly get here?

"Alright but still, she couldn't possibly sail from the opposite side of the continent, so won't she have to fly over the Northern Cities?"

"She could have flown the long way around," Nina suggested.

"Over Firenna *and* Coterra?"

"Yeah, fair point." She nodded.

"What if she just flew north?" I said.

"Around Ellenaria? Maybe, but that'd be a huge waste of fuel."

"Uh, sorry to interrupt, but the simplest solution might be the likeliest," Tobey interjected, "she could have just flown really really high over The Wasteland, that way no one could shoot her down. Not to mention if the plane was outfitted with adequate cloaking or radar deflection technologies they wouldn't even have to worry about The Hoof."

"So we're opening up as a tourist destination now?" I scoffed, "why and how would anyone come here anyway?"

"Well, we *are* the only nation not at war with itself," Nina said.

Fair point.

But still, this exchange program would have to go above the school's jurisdiction and way into the government's. I'd never even heard of a commercial airport so she'd have to come in privately, and in all my years of looking into the sky the only airplanes I'd seen were the fighter jets flown by the nearby military base and the occasional massive one that I guessed was delivering cargo.

I looked over at Tobey who had regained his breath, and found a smile that was so uproariously devilish that I couldn't resist giving him one of my own. I knew what was on his mind. "Think she'll be pretty?"

"By my calculations she will be!" he started, "there's an eighty-four-point-five perc–"

"-Cut to the chase!"

"-there's a good chance she will be, yeah," he said, dejected that I wasn't willing to listen about the percentages stated by whatever censuses cross-referenced with the average genetic sequencing of whatever whatever. "But statistically speaking there's also a good chance that her personality will suck too." He hung his head.

"That's how it usually goes," I sighed and laid back down.

"You guys seriously think that just because a girl is pretty she's mean?" Nina scoffed.

"Tobey said it was statistics," I countered with a grin.

"Yup. Can't fight statistics," he said, sitting on the bench.

"That's why you're so nice, Nina!" I giggled and she slapped my shoulder.

We spent the remainder of lunch-time watching the clouds and trying to see if we could spot a plane carrying a mysterious transfer student somewhere above in that light blue.

Last period went off without a hitch and it wasn't long before Nina and I waved our goodbyes to Tobey, continuing on with our own journey across the waving hills. She stepped with her legs stiff, kicking stones and scuffing her shoes almost as if she was marching. Her book bag bounced off of the back of her legs. She was in a good mood.

I watched her hair sway across her shoulders.

"So... is it okay if I come over?" she asked, and I was kind of taken aback.

"Yeah sure, why do you ask? You're always welcome."

She shrugged, and smiled at me brilliantly. As softly as a fallen leaf.

"You've just been in a funk lately is all."

Had I? I hadn't noticed.

"What are you thinking about?" she queried.

"Uh, not much."

Her smile returned as she answered my unspoken question with a shrug.

"I just like knowing what's on your mind."

My home was a humble two-storey house shaped like an L that my parents had bought maybe... a decade and a half ago. It hung precariously over the edge of a cliff, although I'd convinced myself that the view of the sea was well worth the nightmares of falling into oblivion. I was also its sole tenant for the majority of the time as my parents were off on business trips for years at a time, travelling the world for work. Whatever their 'work' was I couldn't tell you as they never bothered to tell me. Otille had moved out two years ago to study

Literature or something at some big prestigious university on the other side of the country. It was also around then that my parents had last stopped by.

My Mum and Dad had grown up in a dinky little town right on the edge of The Great Plateau, and growing up I'd always wondered why they'd moved. But after going through some of my Mum's stuff I found some newspaper clippings that reported on a series of grisly murders that had taken place when they were kids, so I suppose it was understandable they'd want to move away from a place with a history like that.

I dumped my bag in the foyer and kicked off my shoes before dropping onto the couch, turning the TV on, and flipping over to the Home Network Channel. Nina made herself comfortable at the coffee table by spreading her homework out on its surface and knuckling down, scribbling away in her notebook. After about an hour the TV got boring, and a short channel surf didn't turn up anything interesting to watch so I attempted to fight back boredom by pestering Nina.

"Hey Nina?"

She either didn't hear me or ignored me outright.

"Nina. Ninaaa. Ninaaaaa–"

"-What?" She looked up at me with a glare.

"Wanna play some videogames?"

She scoffed. "No."

"Why not?"

"I'm studying."

"But that looks boring."

"It is," she admitted.

"C'mon." I rolled over and slapped the table, grabbing a book and waving it about. "Play something with me. We can play that one with the boy so I don't absolutely shame you in King of Iron Fist."

"Stop it!" she shouted, reaching for the book I'd snagged, but I could see a smile slowly cracking her shell of seriousness. "All you do is slack off!"

"That's why you like me!" I laughed as I waved the book back and forth, darting between her hands that grabbed at the speed of a snapping turtle's angry bite, and in a moment of daring brilliance she feinted and plucked it out of my hand before I could even realize it.

"You need to get your priorities in order!" she demanded, but her grin betrayed her annoyance and she closed her book. "Go on, set it up! I'll play if you stop annoying me."

With a smile of my own I dusted off my Dad's console and we sat side by side as it whirred to life, groaning and coughing. We used to play fighting games quite often but she got annoyed with losing every match, complaining that I learned all the fighter's moves just to beat her (which isn't exactly my fault, I had nothing better to do), so we began to play story games together instead. As far as I remember we were working on getting through a little game that wasn't particularly hard, but the puzzles wrung my brain dry.

"Maybe move that box over to the window, that one at the far end," Nina said, pointing at the screen.

"Didn't we try that already?"

"No, we tried the window next to it."

"They all look the same," I muttered, but moved the box over anyway. I made the little kid with horns climb up and over it –and huzzah! Nina was right! The last window was the way to go. We'd been stuck on that overgrown balcony looking for the next level for far too long.

"Don't forget to call the girl over."

"Oh right, right," I said, and pressed a button. The boy began yelling back through the window but she wasn't coming. "What's the problem?"

"Maybe she can't get up?" Nina suggested and I climbed back through the window and sure enough she was right again. Standing at the edge of the box he reached down for the girl and she took his hand, then I pulled her up and we walked back through the window. I/he/we held her hand the whole time, making sure not to leave her behind.

"I think it's kinda cute," Nina said.

"What is?"

"That you have to hold her hand. She's so much bigger than him so he's like her brave little knight."

"Yeah I guess you're right. It is cute," I agreed.

I walked with the girl's hand in mine down a crumbling hallway, until it split. Left or right.

I couldn't decide.

"Where should we go?"

Nina shrugged. "You pick."

My grip on the controller got strained. Left or right left or right left or right?

Nina's phone buzzed beside her and she flipped it open then smacked her head. "Oh shoot, sorry, I've gotta go," she said as she stood up. "I forgot about dinner."

"You sure you don't want to just have dinner here?" I suggested.

"I'm sure that everything in your pantry is out of date," she laughed, shoving everything in her book bag. "Don't play any more without me, okay?" she said sternly as she rushed out the door, "see you later!"

I waved goodbye and turned back to the screen only to realize that I was being attacked by a bout of shadowy monsters. Luckily the decision was taken out of my hands as I dispatched my foes quickly, making sure they didn't capture my companion. She was tall and pale, with an almost eerie glow, but she was beautiful too. I'd much rather play as her than the wimpy little kid I was stuck with but hey, at least this way I can hold her hand. Well, I can make *him* hold her hand. This is confusing enough to explain, I thought as I made my way to the couch that served as the 'Save Point'.

Having saved three times just to be sure, I turned the console off and laid down, drowned in the realization that the house was absolutely silent. I laid there for a while, listening to nothing and slowly being crushed by it. Without Nina there it became painfully obvious just how empty my home was. Trying my best to shake off the feeling I got up and walked onto the balcony so I could lean on the railing and marvel at the beauty of the city, but it made me feel more alone than ever. Night had fallen and as such the stars of the city were mirrored by the lights of the sky and together they fought back against the dark.

Chapter Two.

"Silhouettes in the rain."

I decided to not squander the rest of the night watching bad programming, and instead head into town for food. Because as Nina had guessed, everything in my kitchen was way too far out of date to even attempt eating... not unless I fancied a trip to the hospital. The nights were uncharacteristically cold so I changed into something warm and made my way downtown.

The residential area I lived in was quite far up the cliff face, and as such the streets were empty and the lights of the houses were on, shining through the drawn curtains. But the further I made it down the winding lanes and the closer I got to the heart of town, the more lively the city became. For a Wednesday it was surprisingly busy. Cute girls holding signs advertising market stalls waved at rosy-cheeked men dressed in suits who stumbled around off-duty soldiers, preferring to bump into teenagers instead. I recognized a few of the girls waving signs from school, and there were some who were definitely older than they looked. I'd heard that this type of advertising was far more common in the cities, but it had been adopted by families with old cooks and young nieces.

As I walked past a cafe I lazily gazed inwards and saw some of my classmates. Nina was amongst them. She had changed her clothes and brushed her hair (though I saw a few strands of her bed-hair fighting back and remaining wild), and was knee-deep in conversation with a boy whose name I hadn't yet committed to memory. I changed course and ducked down an alleyway, uneager to be noticed as I would undoubtedly be roped into their group activity, however the alleyway I'd turned into had another familiar face waiting for me.

Exhaled smoke stung at my eyes and through my tears I recognized Lucy Lou leaning against a wall.

"Hey," she said.

"Hey," I replied, and took the cigarette from her outstretched hand, noticing a faint red line of lipstick on the filter as I placed it in my mouth. I leaned on the wall opposite her and took a drag. She held her elbows and shivered slightly. She wasn't exactly dressed for the cold.

"I hate these things. I don't know why I smoke them," she said.

"Neither do I," I replied and she laughed lightly.

A few spattering drops of rain began to fall and Lucy ducked beneath an overhead balcony. "So what are you doing here?" she asked. I exhaled a cloud of smoke and she held her hand out, palm up. Droplets landed on her skin as I handed the cigarette back.

"I have the same question."

"I'm waiting for Akera, and you?"

I shrugged. "I didn't feel like cooking so I decided to grab some Otellan."

Looking up past the clothesline and the balconies I saw the stars twinkling behind the clouds and the rain. While the central district had taller buildings, the town itself had mostly been built along the side of a cliff-face. Apparently when they'd built the military base further up the coast they formed a trade-agreement with the little fishing village that had already been there, and soon the fishermen grew wealthy, selling their haul to the soldiers. With good business came opportunity, and with plenty of people travelling from all over the country to take advantage of those opportunities it didn't take long for the village to become a town. By now it had become a really *big* town, and though the population might not have been too impressive, it was compact, so I referred to it as a city. Which I know is technically incorrect, but I don't care.

"Are you sure it's got nothing to do with your *lady friend* over there?" Lucy asked, nodding her head towards Nina. While I readied a dismissive response, time paused. The smoke from Lucy Lou's cigarette hung in the air as she stayed perfectly still, looking at the cafe across the street. As per usual I waited for time to resume, but this time was different. Different to all the other times it had ever paused. I could hear *someone*.

I'm not exactly the curious type, but when a shadow dashed past the back end of the alley I just *had* to follow them. I limped as fast as I could but by the time I reached the mouth of the alley they were already gone, so I had to follow the sounds of their laughter echoing down the back alleys that ran parallel to the main street.

Each neon sign and street light shone through a million raindrops suspended in midair. It felt as if I was traversing through a universe, each raindrop a star. Despite myself I began laughing, enjoying the unique beauty of it all. I quickly became completely drenched, and it was then I saw a silhouette in the rain. For a second I wished I had a camera to capture the image, but I didn't waste any time following the shape through the narrow alleys. It was behind a convenience store that I discovered a second silhouette. They joined together, holding hands as they ran side by side. Hearing the laughter of a girl up ahead I ignored the ache in my leg and carried on. The silhouettes entwined, twirling around one another, but then they split at a junction. One went left, one went right. So I went forward.

I wandered around a little while, lost. This part of town was unfamiliar to me, and it didn't help that I was stumbling around in complete darkness. But then there were approaching footsteps, and the accompanying shadow flitted past across an adjoining lane. I followed suit, chasing the shadow over fences and under drenched clothes hung up on ratty clotheslines. The person I was following was a girl, evidenced by the sweet laughter I'd heard.

She turned, and realizing I was not who she thought I was quickly swerved around a corner. I was hot on her heels as she ran up a flight of stairs onto a rooftop and over to the edge, but I stopped as she leaped across a side street and landed gracefully on the adjacent building. She stopped and turned to face me and waited in the dark.

I hesitantly peeked over the edge to discover that this particular drop was three stories, give or take. I breathed shakily, knowing full well what I was about to do was an absolutely, terribly stupid decision. But knowing that Nina would forever hate me for not trying, I ran the length of the rooftop.

As I kicked off the edge a sharp pain in my right leg caused me to falter and my foot to slip, and I screamed as I flailed in midair; My trajectory no longer sure. My ribcage slammed into the corner of the other rooftop and the wind rushed out of my lungs.

"Please, help!" I gasped as my fingers slid across the slick concrete, failing to find a grip. The girl ran towards me and dived, first grabbing my arm and my collar then pulling as I pushed. Together we managed to haul me up and over the edge, and when I was out of harm's way we both ended up sprawled across the rooftop, breathing heavily and fighting for air.

"Why did you jump, you could have died!" she shouted. Her face was shrouded in darkness, but her voice told me that she was very angry indeed. "Why are you following me?"

"I want... to know who you are..." I wheezed. "How can you... pause time?"

"*You* don't need to know who I am, and ... I don't know how." She got to her feet but my ribs hurt so bad that I decided sitting up would suffice.

"How many of us are there?" I wheezed, checking the condition of my ribcage.

"Counting you, there are three of us that I'm aware of." she answered, walking to the edge of the rooftop. "I don't know who you are. *Don't* follow me again." She dropped off the edge of the building. I crawled over as fast as I could but I only saw her shadow duck into an alleyway. She had dropped down two stories, grappling the fire escape halfway down to break her fall, however I decided to use it for its intended purpose and slowly stepped down. For a moment I considered following her again, using her silhouette, but her tone had conveyed a serious threat that I didn't want to challenge. Instead, I made my way back to Lucy. Halfway through the journey back time had resumed, but I paused it in an instant so that Lucy wouldn't notice my absence. I struggled to remember where I'd been standing before I left.

Lucy turned back to me and confusion was etched on her face. "Sorry, I didn't realize I was standing so close," she said and took a step back. "So why are you hiding from Nina?"

"What?" I scoffed, "I'm not hiding. I just wasn't invited at all."

"That's gotta sting," she hissed. Looking across the street she narrowed her eyes and muttered to herself. "Who's that boy she's with?" Following the rhetorical question was an even more intense squint and a raised eyebrow. "Ohhhhh, I think it's that boy Miyamoto. I've heard he's had a crush on her for a while now. Maybe he's making his move." Then she looked at me and her eyes went wide. "Oh, I'm sorry! I hope I didn't..."

I waved my hand. "Oh no, we're just friends. It's nothing like that."

"Oh, I just see you with her all the time so I just assumed..."

I guess I could see how others might get that idea.

"When did you get so wet?" she asked and as I struggled to come up with an answer she grabbed my sleeve and pulled me under the cover of the balcony. Her query was quickly forgotten though, as she had already turned her attention back to the cafe crowd. I think they were her old crowd.

"Why don't you go over and say hi?"

She shook her head. "Nuh uh, there's no way I could do that. I'm pretty sure they all hate me."

"They're your old friends right? I'm sure they'd be happy to see you again."

She looked at them, lips tightly pressed together. The fierce determination on her face was almost cute. "Okay fine, I'll go over. If you come with me."

Oh heck no, I sure as hell didn't want that. What if they made me part of the group and I had to hang out with them regularly?

"Jeez, you don't have to make a face like *that*," she said, hitting my arm. "I'm only kidding anyway. I'm still meeting with Akera, remember?" Then, by some twist of fate her phone chirped and she flicked it open to find a message from Akera telling her she couldn't make it.

"She always does this..." she sighed, flicking her phone closed. Her face fell then, all her features revealing a thinly held fatigue. I had never seen Lucy without a smile on her face and I couldn't handle it. Unable to bear the pained expression she held, I grabbed her hand and led her across the street, and though she protested she wanted to get out of the rain even more. The door jingled, signaling our arrival, and Nina along with her friends looked over to see us completely drenched. They laughed, but beckoned us over with welcoming smiles. Nina's eyes moved down to our intertwined hands and just for a moment I saw an expression that I couldn't quite explain, but it was replaced by a tight smile by the time we sat down.

Immediately they offered us warm drinks and a tablecloth to dry off with. All of the group were smiling at Lucy, asking her questions about her family and how she'd been. At first she was shy, but gradually she warmed up and it was like they'd never been apart; laughing at inside jokes and catching her up on the gossip she'd missed out on. I, however, was very unfamiliar with this group of friends Nina had, so I leaned back and drank my tea in silence. I did recognize a few of them as School Council members, but the others were completely new to me. I guess they were in the grade above or something.

After an hour or so later, the group began to disband. Lucy waved as she headed home with two other girls and Nina approached me.

"Are you okay? You've been holding your side funny," she said, her tone like a rock.

"Yeah no, I should be okay. Don't worry." I waved a hand, dismissing her worry but she poked a finger into my ribs and I howled in pain. She immediately flinched and began apologizing.

"Are you sure you're okay?"

"Yes, I'm fine!" I hissed.

"Sorry..." She looked unsure. "So, uh, Miyamoto and Suzu I are going the long way home so we could grab some ice-cream from that new shop in town. I was gonna ask if you wanted to come, but do you need me to help you get home?"

"No thanks, I should be fine. Go with them. Have fun."

"Are you sure?"

"Yes! Now go!" I said as I stood, but the pain in my chest caused me to shout.

"Okay... sure thing," she replied. "I guess I'll see you tomorrow then. Goodnight."

And with that she walked away.

Seeing her go I felt something tug within my chest, and it wasn't the injured ribs. I considered running after her, but she was already gone and I'd already said what I'd said. I cursed myself and started the long journey home. On the way I thought about the Time-Pausing girl. She had inferred she had an accomplice, if their silhouettes dancing together hadn't made that clear enough. I wondered how many of us were out there, it couldn't be just us three, right? There was also the question of her identity. From the sound of her voice and the size of her, I deduced that she was around my age, but there was a fifty-fifty chance that the high-school she attended was mine.

My mind went back to Nina.

To how her face looked after I shouted at her.

Picture a man with a baseball bat standing right behind me, and swinging it so hard that my head snapped off and I wasn't there anymore. Every time I embarrassed myself, or felt guilt, I imagined him standing behind me, and tonight I wanted him to swing. Swing it!

I took a breath.

Get home, put on Heavy Doorah's Wrestling Highlights, try not to remember, try not to think. Definitely do *not* think about how hurt and dejected Nina looked. Watch the masked man wrestle, and try to make it through this night.

Chapter Three
"The girl from Europa."

I slept through my alarms but woke to a text from Nina telling me she'd gone early to meet the transfer student, and that I shouldn't wait for her. I rushed to get ready but still found myself arriving halfway through Homeroom, and while Mr. Washy gave me a stern look reminiscent of an angry goldfish, I wasn't otherwise punished. Soon I found myself reclined in my seat, yawning as I relaxed when my phone vibrated in my pocket. I made sure Mr. Washy was looking elsewhere as I brought my phone out, flipping it open under the desk. The header told me it was a text from my sister, but the text she'd sent sent a cold shiver down my spine.

[I think I must be psychic]

Instantly my mind began to race, thinking that if both she and I had powers maybe it was genetic or something... but then that would mean our parents had powers too. I shuddered at the thought.

[What makes you say that?] I replied, furiously clicking at the numpad and staring at the screen for minutes until she replied.

[I was just thinking of you and then you texted me! Crazy, I know!]

I raised my eyebrow but sure enough I had sent her a string of incoherent letters and numbers. A 'pocket text'. No doubt sent when I was mashing the keys, desperately trying to kill my alarm.

[Sorry, pocket text]

[Thought so, now get back to work!]

I shook my head and pocketed my phone, and looking up came face to face with Mr. Washy. He peered at me from behind his spectacles and tutted disapprovingly while bobbing his head.

"First late, now messing around on your phone. Surely if you can divert all of your attention away from my teachings you must have learnt this subject already, correct?" He turned away and walked back to the blackboard. "So!" He said with a slap of his ruler against the board. "Explain the answer to this question!"

I tried to read the writings on the board but the scribblings were incomprehensible to me. A mash of numbers and letters not unlike the message I'd sent to my sister. It had been months since I'd even looked at my maths book, let alone opened it! On a side note, since when were we being taught algebra in Homeroom? My eyes darted down to my book and the empty lines, then back up at the board, then finally across the faces of my classmates. Upon each was a smug smile. They knew me, and they knew I didn't know the answer. But I thank the Goddesses above for Tobey, as the angel himself had his sketchpad open and tilted in my direction, giving me the answer and saving my soul!

"Uh.. well sir, personally I'd have to go with... forty-seven? Yes! When you divide X by pi with a factorial of three-hundred-and-twenty to the power of eight, you get forty-seven degrees with a remainder of two!"

(Don't ask me to explain what any of this means. I had never even read most of those words until that exact moment.)

Mr. Washy stood slightly straighter, although his expression did not soften until quite suddenly a smile broke the surface. "Very well done my boy! What a surprise!" He clapped his hands and spun in a circle. "I'll be expecting great things from you in the upcoming exams! But please refrain from texting in my class."

"No problem sir." I said, giving him a hesitant smile, knowing he was going to be very disappointed when the time came.

The bell awoke me, interrupting a rather enjoyable dream I struggle to remember, and I joined Tobey on our usual pilgrimage to the rooftop. Today he was flipping through the pages of a girls fashion magazine. The same one Lucy Lou and Akera had been discussing.

"Don't you find these trends intriguing?"

Not particularly.

"In each design and outfit, they accentuate the color of the season, right?" He said, showing me pictures to emphasize his point. "Right now short sleeves and breathable materials are the go, due to the heat and all which is perfectly understandable, but have you noticed it yet?"

Noticed what, exactly?

"In each and every female fashion design, not just here but prevalent in office and school too, is the exposure of the knees! What do you think of that?"

I gave him an odd look but he was so absorbed in his thoughts he didn't register it.

"If I were to follow the common trends of humanity, would that mean that knees are nothing to be thought about? A common sight because they bring nothing to the enjoyment of the passerby? Or, is it because of its constant appearance, that the knee is the most desirable aspect of the female body?"

I snatched the magazine from his hands and slapped the back of his head with it, scowled at him as he rubbed his noggin. "You've got a problem man, you're always running your mouth! People are giving us odd looks you know!" He sulked but I sighed and shook my head as I turned to walk away.

"Wait!" he hissed, and I rolled my eyes but walked back to where he stood at the window gazing inwards to the willow tree.

"What?"

"There!" Tobey jabbed at the glass window with a finger, "There, do you see it?"

I leaned from one side to the other, squinting through the glass until I saw a cat perched on a window sill a floor below us. Nondescript. Calico. Was it somebody's pet? Were we even allowed pets on campus? "Huh."

"It's been following me for days now." Tobey muttered, sneering at the cat who just calmly licked a paw.

"It's just a cat."

"It's not just any cat. That calico has been on my trail for a week at least. There was a grey one the week before, and a tortoiseshell the week before that."

I rolled my eyes. Only Tobey would have some ongoing rivalry with a gang of felines. And only he would even think a cat would be bothered to follow him. "Come on," I said, and slapped the back of his head. "Let's not keep Nina waiting any longer."

We continued our journey only to find Oscar around the corner, standing above a girl with one hand on a wall caging her in like a butterfly in a matchbox. The stance he'd taken would easily be explained away by saying: "No sir, I saw her crying and decided to comfort her." I knew him.

I couldn't hear his words but I saw his lips moving, and worse till I could see the corners of his mouth turned upwards a millimetre. I really didn't want to step in, but I knew that dealing with Oscar alone wasn't the best feeling in the world. I did what anyone would do and swallowed my fear, approaching with one hand out and placing it on his shoulder. "Hey man, let's give her some space, okay?" I said, and in a flash his hand was around my wrist, twisting it painfully. I gasped as he forced my hand back, and leaned in close, his voice low. Eyes ice cold.

"Are you finally stepping up to the plate?"

His question confused me for a moment, and I didn't know what to say so the words choked in my throat as he grinned from ear to ear. As I begged for something to come out my mouth we both heard the sound of rapidly approaching footsteps. Turning at the same time we came to see a boy running towards us at full speed.

"Get away from her!" he yelled as he brought his fist back, leaping into the air as he did so. It was then I felt a hand on the small of my back, and a push, and all of a sudden I was greeting the stranger's knuckles with my face.

An explosion of pain launched me off my feet and I fell backwards, first hitting the wall and spinning before landing hard on the ground and winding myself. I gasped in agony, desperate for air as I writhed on the floor, my ribs stinging again. Blood was spilling torrentially from my nose; I could tell from the feeling of a wet warmth spreading across my cheeks and over my lips. Shoes scuffed across the wooden floor, squeaking loudly as the two wrestled. I couldn't see anything through the instinctual tears, and Tobey pulled me away as I wiped my eyes, smudging blood across my cheeks in the process. I watched as Oscar flipped his assailant over his leg and sent a snaking fist into his face, silencing him.

I was astounded by the amount of blood that was pouring from my nose, and disturbed by the sick smile on Oscar's face as he sent another fist down. I called out weakly and he looked over to stare into my eyes as he readied another punch. I wanted to urge Tobey to do something, to help, but words still evaded me and Tobey didn't stand much of a chance either. As Oscar launched his fist a hand grabbed his forearm, stopping the assault. He turned, ready to send a punch into the face of his new opponent but he stopped when he realized it was David.

Oscar wrenched his hand from David's grip and straightened his collar. The two stood eye-to-eye, staring each other down. David's rage was barely contained and I saw his fists balled and his jaw tight, but Oscar stood with a smug expression, challenging him. While the two of them were of similar height, David was much stronger, and I think Oscar knew this too.

"Now David, I'm not sure you were there at the start to see exactly what transpired, but I'm sure if you were aware of the circumstances even you would agree that this is merely self-defense."

David's anger materialized in an aura of boiling steam, but he restrained himself. I was amazed at his self-control, honestly. If I was in his shoes Oscar would be a smear.

"I don't care what you call it, Oscar. Get out of here."

Oscar stared. I could sense some semblance of understanding cross his face, but it was less of a respectful look and more of an analysis of an opponent. I didn't see what I'd been hoping for. Fear.

Oscar dusted his shoulders. "Right. I'll be on my way. No harm no foul, right?" he said with a sly grin, slightly turned up at the corners; A smile only I could see. David crouched by the boy's side and shook him gently, and I heard him cough a response. The girl, who had been slumped against the wall, crying, rushed to his side and held him.

"Damn bro, he messed you up." David said as he knelt beside me.

"Actually it was him," I said, pointing at the boy and laughing at David's reaction, then wincing at the immediate pain. "No worries though, it was a genuine mistake." Tobey helped me lean against the wall and I pinched my nose in an attempt to restrict the blood flow. I spat blood. David went back to the pair, making sure they were fine. He suggested we go to the office and tell the teachers what had happened, but we all refused. He reasoned that because there were five witnesses, and too many injuries for the teachers to ignore, that they'd take action. David eventually realized that he was getting nowhere and gave up, returning to me.

"You'll tell the teachers, right?"

I shook my head. "Nah, it'd be no use. Those two would deny everything, and so would Oscar. There's also the fact that he *did* throw the first punch," I said, motioning to the boy. "And because the Owens are a big sponsor for the school, it means that there's no way they'd lose that big money over a 'petty squabble.'"

I knew exactly what would happen.

The truth of Kou Funi's expulsion was often lost in retellings and rumours, but I was close enough to that fire to feel the flames. Or rather I knew the firestarter. I coughed, and more blood spilled out of my nose.

At least I now had an excuse to miss out on History.

The boys helped me up and escorted me to the nurse's office, and upon entering the clinic Nurse Singer smiled at Tobey, wheeling out a life size anatomy half-organ man.

"Mr. Takeru! Back to continue our lessons?"

David and I shared a look.

As I sat across from Eileen I watched in amusement as her eyes widened in shock, and she gasped as a droplet of blood decided to vacate my nasal canal, dripping onto my shirt.

"Oh. My. Goodness... what happened to you?" The expression of pure concern in her voice elevated my condition for a moment.

"Our friend here tried to get to second base with Nurse Singer," Tobey joked, but Eileen just scowled at him.

"He wouldn't do that, he's much more of a gentleman than you!" Her defense of my reputation made my heart flutter.

"Sometimes they like 'em bad," Tobey muttered to himself.

"I got punched as a reward for helping a victim of Oscar's," I explained, and she got up, walking around the table and wrapping her arms around me.

I was in heaven. Her perfume... ah, strawberries...

"You poor thing! I can't believe Oscar did this to you." she said, rubbing my head.

"He didn't do it directly..." David muttered, looking away.

We explained exactly what had happened and the whole time she called me brave and stroked my hair. To be in this position I would have been punched twice, maybe even three times.

"You have to tell the teachers," Eileen said.

"I tried telling him that but he won't listen," David said with a shrug of his shoulders. I gave her the same reasoning that I gave David and while she wasn't happy with it, she at least understood my hesitancy. The rest of Study Hall was spent talking, and we got told off by the librarian more than once. Not that it mattered. When the bell finally rang I felt my soul split in two as Eileen untangled herself from me, but I was grateful for even a small blessing.

I didn't have the energy for a long walk so we made our way directly to the roof, and we found Nina already there sitting with who I assumed was the transfer student. Their conversation quieted as they looked at my newly beaten visage, and Nina was instantly on her feet with her hands on my face making a fuss and asking all sorts of questions.

"Are you okay? What happened? Who did this to you? Where does it hurt? Are you okay?"

"Why's your hair so messy?" Tobey pondered aloud, and Nina yelled "Shut up!" so fiercely he recoiled like a kicked dog, sulking and completely ignored as she turned back to me, hands on either side of my face. Her gaze was serious, and she looked from one eye to the other.

"Who did this to you? I'll kill them."

I laughed painfully.

"So this is your... *boyfriend*?" Asked an exotic accent that drew heavily on the vowels. Nina bashfully turned around and I looked over her shoulder, instantly stunned by just how beautiful the transfer student was, with tanned skin of an olive complexion and long hair as black as the night that hung playfully over her equally dark eyes. "This is who you were talking about, no?"

She was talking about me?

"Er, uh, no. Well, yes. I was talking about him, but no, he's not my boyfriend," Nina stammered as she stepped away.

"What she said," I added and followed suit.

The foreigner's lilting laugh came beautifully, like a harp being plucked.

"Of course not. Sorry, it is just that you were so... *pathmeonada*... Is everyone here so close?" she asked, seemingly sincerely, but her eyes betrayed a sense of mischief.

"Yes," answered Tobey, "I'd be happy to show you."

"Not really," Nina quickly corrected with an elbow thrown into his ribs. "We've just known each other for ages, is all."

The foreigner stood and walked over to us, hopping from one foot to the other with such grace it was as if she was floating. Her long hair swung lavishly, and she made the school uniform look like it belonged on a runway. Coming to a stop in front of us she grinned darkly, her smile making both Tobey and I weak in the knees.

"So if *you* aren't his romantic partner," she said, giving a rather fake smile to Nina. "Is he available?"

Nina's face went bright red as she looked away, and I gave a humorless chuckle.

"I'm uh, not looking, but I suppose I am. Single, that is," I answered, scratching the back of my head.

Someone save me from this hell!

"I am!" Tobey piped up.

"Brilliant!" Clapped the foreigner, ignoring Tobey. "In that case, may I have your... *arithnumous*?" she said, holding up her phone.

I raised an eyebrow. "Oh you mean *number*, right." I looked at Nina but I couldn't see her expression, so with great hesitancy I flipped open my mobile and read the number to her aloud, and when she struggled to understand I took the phone from her and keyed it in myself, accidentally brushing her hand with mine.

"You are my first," the foreigner said with a sultry tone that made me blush and Tobey collapse. My phone chirped and looked down at the screen.

[treat me well xx] came a text from an unknown number.

"Uh, what's your name?" I asked, filling out the contact.

“Apronas Isabella Ulani Ella Ofella Su Mendacion,” she said, “but you can call me Apronas.” Batting her eyelids she reached her hand out in an old-timey handshake I’d only seen in movies. The type where you kiss their hand. Oh what the hell, maybe it's normal in her culture? With a hot face I closed my eyes and kissed the soft skin of her hand, and looking up I saw Nina staring at me like I was a bug she was very eager to crush.

“Your name,” she purred, “it is not too dissimilar to the God of Time in my culture. You might have heard of Oenos, no?”

“That’s not similar at all,” I muttered, but she shook her head and grabbed my arm.

“If I miss my country too much I shall simply say your name, and I will feel at home,” she whispered with a dramatic flair, no doubt making Tobey jealous.

“You do that...” I sighed, resigned to the angry looks I knew Nina would be throwing my way, and the servitude I had been forced into.

“Have I seen you somewhere before?” Tobey asked and Apronas whirled around to face him, squinting. She cocked her head.

“No,” she said with a stern tone.

Tobey reached his hand out and she turned her nose up at him, like he smelt bad or something. I hadn’t noticed any pungent odors emanating from my bespectacled friend, so her reaction was more than unusual. Even more odd was the fact that as she took his hand her body shuddered, but only slightly. It was such a small movement I’m sure she had practiced keeping it concealed. All of the warmth she had shown me, however false-hearted it was, was not given to him. He seemed to take no notice, but as he turned away I swore she sniffed the air, and the sun glinted in her eyes like golden stardust that was gone so soon I couldn’t be sure I’d ever seen it at all.

Thankfully the conversation fell into relative normality, saved by Nina who was back to her usual self and bombarding the poor girl with questions about her home country's climate, the national food dishes, what technology was available, its history and all different queries about the culture. Apronas answered them all with finesse, and we learnt that she was from a warm country in the southern Europan Province called Urlou which held bull runs –the concept of which rather intrigued Nina– and that they'd kept the ruins of ancient cities in good care, so old towers and columns dotting the countryside within the cities still stood tall.

How she withstood Nina's constant barrage of inquiry I have no idea, although I would have to applaud the strength of her character.

That was the first time I heard the name Oenos, but back then I had no idea just how much it would matter in the coming years.

I was on the couch watching TV when I'd gotten a text so I flipped my phone open and was greeted by a message letting me know that Nina would be over with dinner. In hungry anticipation I turned on the kettle and began reading a magazine as I waited for it to boil, but I soon became so engrossed in hot celebrity drama that I was startled by Nina barging through the front door with plastic bags in both hands.

"You gonna help with this?" she called out, grunting as she put a bag down on the inner step.

I leapt off the couch to greet her. "Sorry," I lamely apologized, picking up the bags and taking them to the kitchen while she sat down and took her shoes off. There was quite a bounty, and it was heavy too. It was no wonder she'd been struggling with it. "Why'd you get so much?"

"I think it was the chef's birthday or something. They were singing and there were decorations up, they gave me extra food as thanks for being a regular." she said, walking into the kitchen. She patted my shoulder. "Move, I'll get it ready. I'm afraid of what you'd do to it."

I stared at her.

"Okay," she giggled, "why don't you make us some tea or something?"

"Sure," I conceded. Her fears were well placed.

While she dished our food out into plates and bowls, I was by her side, expertly and deftly concocting a pot of tea. I had once bought a Miss. Morina Winslow DVD from TV that showed how to make tea like a teamaster, or like our ancestors did, and I learnt all the steps off by heart.

Nina aired out her shirt with one finger pulling at the collar but her clothing stuck to her skin, no doubt owing to the ticky sheen of sweat coating her body. She had most likely come from Track Club and ran straight from there to the Otellan Beef store and to mine. I remember when I had stamina like hers.

In an attempt to fend off her intoxicating aroma I grabbed one of the bowls of sauced meat she had prepared and shoved it below my nose, and though I tried my hardest to allow the scent of stewed beef and its accompanying spices to fill my lungs, all it did was sting my nose.

"Are you okay? You're acting a little funny," she said, stepping closer and rubbing her thumb softly over my nose.

My heartrate must have tripled.

I nodded and she gave me a pitiful smile, retracting her hand.

"Let's have some eats, yeah?" I said, putting the bowl down and grabbing the teapot and its paraphernalia. With a return trip from both of us our feast was prepared, resting on the coffee table; a meal fit for kings. Or, I guess a king and a queen in this instance. We even had entertainment. No jester sadly, but the TV would do.

We began arguing over whether Enricho should remain in a relationship with the strict but beautiful Ms. Colionne, or follow his heart and run after his fanciful lover Isabella when Nina spilled some sauce on her shirt and groaned in annoyance.

"No worries. Just grab one of my shirts," I said.

"Oh, thanks," she replied and stood up, making her way into my room, quickly returning with a shirt in hand.

"Why is your window always open?" she asked, pointing a thumb over her shoulder. "I don't think I've ever seen it closed."

"It's in case someone needs to get in."

"And they can't just use the front door?"

"To some people the front door is a foreign concept," I answered and she shrugged, adequately satisfied with that unsatisfying answer. Kneeling down she looked over at the TV and lifted her shirt over her head.

"Is it good?" she asked as she exposed her pale, flat stomach. In an instant my face became hot to the touch and I spun around, looking at the wall and admiring its craftsmanship.

"Uh, yeah. O-of course."

What was she doing!?

I wasn't prepared for this!

What is she even referring to? The food, I hope...

"Apronas was... *awfully friendly*, wasn't she?" Nina said with a scowl as I heard the stained shirt hit the floor. I tried to keep my gaze trained on the bookcase and my mind distracted by reading the titles of the books, but knowing that just behind me was Nina rather... lacking in clothing, to put it one way, was making me feel dizzy.

"Maybe her culture is just like that," I reasoned, "it could be normal for her."

I heard her grunt as she stretched, and sigh as the tension was released.

My nose started bleeding.

"Maybe," Nina agreed, grabbing the clean shirt. Then she was silent for a moment.

I think realization set in.

"Wait, did I just-"

"-Yes you did." I preemptively answered.

"Why didn't you say anything!" she hollered, and I felt something collide with the back of my head. Her shirt had been her weapon and I picked it up as I turned around, trying to ignore how warm it was. She was now fully clothed but her face was as red as mine, although I'm guessing hers was red due to anger.

"I thought you were doing it on purpose!" I yelled, throwing the shirt back. Nina ducked beneath it and readied a plastic spork as her new weapon.

"Why would I.. *strip,* on purpose!?" she yelled and threw the spork at me, although all it did was harmfully bounce off my shoulder. She then froze, and crawled towards me on her hands and knees with her fists pounding the floor, and I tried to back away but she was too fast and grabbed me by the collar, yanking my head forward. Her face was dark, and her eyes stared at me with a glare that could kill. "You didn't Pause... did you?"

I shook my head vehemently. "O-of course not! I saw more than enough..."

Nina gawked and slapped me, then she looked at her hand, then the floor.

"Ew, you're bleeding everywhere, you perv!"

The episode ended on a cliffhanger which would only be resolved the following Thursday, and we both groaned in agony. Throwing fists into cushions and cursing vehemently.

"They always do this!"

"I need to know what happened *now*!" Nina cried, "this is torture!"

I patted her back and she sighed, her shoulders falling. "We just have to make it one week, Nina. Just seven more more nights and we'll get our answers. Be strong!" I said and she bolstered her strength enough to jump to her feet and shake her fist valiantly at the sky.

"Just one week!" she chanted. But as she calmed down she asked for my wrist, and upon turning it over she hissed upon seeing the time. "Oh, shoot. It's getting late. I should probably get going," she said, then looking around at the food I saw a solemn look at her face.

"Don't worry about the mess, I'll clean it," I said, waving a hand. "*Or*, you could help clean and just stay over if you want," I yawned, reclining on the couch. "It *is* pretty late, and I do technically live closer to school."

She stood above me and winked. "Maybe next time."

I blushed.

Definitely *not* what I meant.

She grabbed her belongings and refused my offer to walk her home, so I was left with an empty house, and it was only long after she'd left that I realized I had forgotten to tell her about the other Time Pausers. But I had dishes to clean and a bed to sleep in which were far more important, at least to me. Facing the flowing curtains of the open window I could see the moon shining brilliantly beyond. Her light quiet and pale. Mere moments from sleep I heard my phone buzz, and with a groan I flipped it open, squinting as the bright screen attacked my retinas.

[are you still awake?] The message read. At first I thought it was from Nina or my sister, but then I realized it was from Apronas. Why was she messaging me so late? Maybe she was struggling to sleep or something.

[trying to sleep, what do you need?] I responded, and ten seconds later my phone rang. Ugh. I rolled my eyes and gritted my teeth. I really did *not* want to talk.

"Hello?"

"Good evening, that is how you say it, no?" Apronas giggled from the other end of the line. "I am wanting to meet tomorrow after school, you can show me places in the town."

"What about Nina?" I asked.

"What *about* Nina?" she replied. I didn't like the intonation she used.

"You can go to all the girly stores with her," I barked, closing my eyes and turning away from the window.

"I'd rather go with you."

"Why?"

"I want to make someone blush," she said breathily.

"So take Tobey."

"No!" she hissed, then quickly she gained her composure. "Stop playing so hard to get, Oenos. I am meeting you tomorrow after school."

I rubbed my eyes. Nina couldn't get mad at me, it was *her* friend I was helping. Besides, I had a feeling that saying 'yes' was the only way to get her to stop bothering me.

"Sure," I muttered, and she giggled.

"Dream of me," she whispered, and the line went dead.

Devil woman.

Chapter Four
"Don't call it a date!"

Waking up was a punishment that I believed was undeserved. My broken nose was stuffy and my eyes had been puffing up in response, not to mention ribs that were aching like nobody's business. I just tried to smile at the me in the mirror and take it as a sign that I was healing, but the gruesome smile that was returned didn't do much to bolster my confidence.

I was already late to school so I treated the hike more like a stroll, and I was surprised to find Tobey waiting for me by my locker, holding my shoes. How long had he been waiting? I don't ever remember giving him my locker code, but I didn't question him.

"Tut-tut-tut." He shook his head. "Late again, O-boy?" he said as I took the pair from him, trying to change into them as painlessly as I could. "You're hopeless without Nina chasing you out of bed!"

"I'm trying man, give me some credit at least..." I muttered, hopping on one foot. "Why are you here?"

"Why not?" He shrugged. "Anyway, I'll catch you later. I'm joining Ms. Kurin on a stamina-building exercise."

"The gym teacher?"

"Yep."

"We don't have P.E., do we?"

"*You* don't." He grinned, waving goodbye and leaving me to trip on a loose shoelace and land face-first into a locker door. Once I made it out the other end of the battle and survived, I began making my way to class. It wasn't long though until I came across Lucy Lou and Akera ambling through the halls. Akera was talking loudly but Lucy was trying to ignore her, attempting to read a rather large book.

"Mornin'. What are you two skipping?"

"Geography," answered Akera, clicking away at the buttons of her phone.

"Math, although I really should be there," Lucy said glancing at Akera.

"No, you shouldn't. It's just a waste of time."

"Akera..." Lucy's voice pleading. "I'll fail my test."

"Test? Since when did you care about tests?" Akera scoffed.

"Since... It doesn't matter when!" Lucy protested.

"Lucy," I interjected, not wanting to hear even more bickering. "You and I share math together right? You can come with me."

Akera slammed her phone shut and glared at me. The reverberating crack of her cell echoed throughout the halls and caused a tense silence.

"You're not even going to do anything so don't force her to go with you." She tilted her head. "What happened to your face?"

"Actually... I want to go," Lucy mumbled, and Akera turned to stare at her. I could tell that just beneath her skin was bubbling molten lava, boiling red hot rage. Shaking she flicked her phone open and turned away, furiously clicking away at the numpad. "Whatever, Lucy. Go."

We hesitated for only a moment, but that moment earned us an angry glare. Together we hurried away and behind us we heard her call out: "Lucy, I won't be seeing you after school. I'm busy." Upon hearing that the girl at my side deflated. We almost made it to class before she stopped and sighed.

"I know it's stupid, but she makes me feel guilty for wanting to go to class," she admitted. "She's my best friend, but sometimes she's a lot to handle alone."

I couldn't tell why she was telling me of all people. I sighed, knowing I'd have to come up with something reasonable to say. This was definitely not what I wanted to be dealing with, and I certainly didn't want to say anything bad about Akera, lest it reached her ears and I found myself the target of her rage. In the end I said something completely out of character.

"I think that you should do what you think is best for *you*, Lucy. Akera might be your best friend, but having an education could mean a lot for your future."

Bah! Education? Me? Never. All of this was said with borrowed confidence, but she nodded earnestly in return.

"Thanks," she said, giving me a smile so bright it softened my edges just the littlest bit. "You're so wise."

Whatever you say.

"Oh stop it," I laughed.

"Hey, you two! Get to class!" A voice shouted from down the corridor.

We looked at eachother then ran.

We were of course very late, but the teacher decided to go easy on us. Probably out of disbelief that we showed up at all. Thankfully nothing of interest happened and I was able to have a nap, undisturbed, listening to the scribblings of Lucy trying to catch up. On my way to my next class as I stretched I passed the boy from yesterday atop a stepladder, hanging up a poster with a muffin on it. He had a black eye too, but more bruising on his jaw. The cut on his lip was still bright red.

"Hey." I waved, and he nodded at me before turning his attention back to the poster. *How curt.* Did he not recognize me? No, the black eyes and red nose were a dead giveaway, he was the one who caused them after all! When he noticed I hadn't left he looked at me, eyebrow raised expectantly.

"Yes?"

Crap. I wasn't sure why I was standing here either.

"What's with the posters?" I asked, pointing at the paper in his hand meekly.

"They're for a baking event. You can read, right?"

Rude.

He sighed.

"I'm part of the school committee," he said, answering a question I hadn't asked. "You can help if you want."

I shook my head. "I can't right now. I'm free at lunch though."

He stepped down from the little ladder then handed me four rolled up posters and a stick of gum. "That's for hanging them up," he explained, then climbed back up the ladder and continued hanging up the first one. "Put them up around the music room would you?"

I felt a lump in my throat.

First this guy punches me and doesn't apologize, then he's rude to me and now I'm stuck doing his labor. What exactly had led to this turn of events?

The bell rang and I cursed, dreading being late again.

Mr. Obeno shook his head as I entered but did nothing more, and I made my way to the table next to the window only to discover that I had a desk-mate that wasn't Tobey. Now to quickly explain, most of the classes had single-person desks but a few had tables for multiple people to share, and today I would be sharing it with *her* as Tobey was apparently busy. I sighed and trudged over, trying to ignore the devilish grin she gave me.

"*Lucky me,*" she whispered, "*I was unaware we were to share a class.*"

"*Aren't you supposed to share your classes with Nina?*" I whispered back, placing my book on the desk so it at least looked like I was studying.

"*The scholtad... er, power facility, decided to put me here. Perhaps to encourage making new friends. Like yourself.*"

I frowned. Power facility?

The door slid open, interrupting my train of thought and I watched as Tobey entered the class, greeted by a smile and a wave from Mr. Obeno. Where was this hospitality with me? Grinning to himself

Tobey walked towards us, but as he saw Apronas by my side he cursed himself, clenching his fists and shaking them at the sky before resigning himself to his fate... The empty seat next to Gongil Minnows. A large fellow who was, how to put this politely? Not the nicest smelling person you would ever meet.

I returned my attention to the conversation at hand.

"*Do you mean school faculty?*"

"*Do they have a facility of power?*" She asked in return.

She had me there.

All throughout the next hour she asked me about the different words Mr. Obeno was teaching us, like what they meant and how they were pronounced. What were the proper present and negative tense usages for them. I tried my best to help but I got lost very quickly, realizing just how little I knew about my own mother tongue. Eventually the bell rang and I was saved from having to try and explain what 'gastro-economical' meant. I gathered my things and joined the crowd leaving the room.

"What's with the posters?" Eileen asked, having appeared out of thin air.

"I'm uh, helping out some guy on the committee or something..." I answered distractedly, looking for Apronas. There was a break in the crowd and I saw her being pestered by Tobey. She had a scowl on her face and he was gleefully showing her a magazine.

I hope he wasn't talking about knees again.

"That's very unlike you." Eileen's tone teased, pulling me back into the conversation. "Want some help?" she asked as she looped her arm around mine.

I wasn't about to refuse help from *Eileen*, but upon remembering the destination deigned by the boy I gladly accepted, wholly, entirely, and desperately accepted. I would need all the moral support I could get. We made our way down a floor and stopped on the landing to hang up a poster. Both she and I had begun chewing the packet of gum, blowing giant bubbles as we went.

"So who are you helping anyway? Is it a girl?" she teased.

"Funnily enough, it was the guy who did *this*." I said, pointing at my face.

"Getting bullied into hanging up posters, that's a new one," she giggled. "Speaking of, your face is looking better."

"You lie." I pushed on the last corner of the poster and we carried on.

"So... I need some advice." Eileen asked shyly, twirling some hair around her finger and avoiding looking at my face. "It's about my little sister."

Why did everyone need *my* help today?

"You do realize I don't have a kid sister of my own, right?" I replied as we stopped to hang up a second one. Turns out, it was indeed an advertisement for a charity baking event. It also happened to coincide with the school's 'Athletics Celebration Day' coming up the Monday after next.

Ironic.

"So what's the problem anyway?" I asked, against my better judgement.

"So, there's this competition she wants to join, right? But she tells me there's no point. She says that she'll just lose so it defeats the purpose in trying." She paused for a moment to help push the top of the poster against the wall. "What should I say to her?"

"What competition is it?" I asked.

"Uh, Chess?" she answered, though it sounded more like a guess.

I had the feeling she wasn't really talking about her sister but I didn't want to assume anything if I was wrong, which was more often than not. I spent a few seconds thinking of what to say with my tongue stuck out, trying to stop the top corners from peeling off the wall.

"Tell her... seize the day, or something like that." With the corners firmly stuck in place I turned to look at Eileen. Her long hair was beautifully brushed today, and bundled through a hairclip on the top of her head. Eager for my response she smiled at me patiently, eyes blinking like butterflies from behind her glasses. "There's always a chance so why not take it, right? Besides, it might end up being just some plain old fun. That's the most important part anyway."

Man, I could tell just how lame it sounded as it passed my lips but it made her smile softly.

"Thanks. That's a good answer. You almost sounded cool," she giggled.

I shook my head but cherished the compliment and turned the corner. I halted and my brain froze all at once upon seeing the sign for the music room up above the door.

"Uh, say, Eileen? Could you please do me a favor?"

"Okay. What do you need?"

I looked at her, but couldn't hold her gaze and dropped my eyes to the floor. "Could you please hang this poster up over there?"

"Sure thing," she said, giving me an odd look as she walked away with the poster in hand. I pulled my phone out and thumbed through the settings, trying to ignore staring eyes and keep myself occupied as I waited for her return.

"Okay, we're all done," Eileen said, smiling and dusting her hands off.

"Awesome, thanks for the help."

"Are you okay? You look like you've seen a ghost," she asked, tilting her head and looking into my eyes. I didn't know if I should say anything.

"Yeah, I'm okay, don't worry about me. I just had some bad breakfast I think," I lied with a smile. "Where are you off to?"

"I'm gonna head to the Literature Club room."

"Huh. I didn't know you were part of that club."

"Yeah," she shrugged, "I was gonna be a librarian but some other girl got the job first. I still get to read though, so that's nice."

"I suppose so. I'm gonna go see Nina now, I guess."

"Aww, you don't wanna read books with me?"

"'Not exactly," I chuckled, rubbing the back of my head. "Your kind of books are far too advanced for me."

"Your choice," she winked, "I'll see you later. Bye!"

"Bye!" I waved, watching her skip away. I wanted to get to Nina as soon as I could, and luckily I was right next to a fire escape. So I made my... *escape*.

Get it?

Anyway, sitting right outside with a scowl on her face and a cigarette in her lips was Akera. I closed the window behind me and leaned on the railing. The air was cool thanks to a breeze, and the boys kicking balls in the field were in a good mood. The ocean waves lapped lazily at the beach front far below.

"Hey," I said.

"Get lost," she muttered in reply.

"A little hospitality would be nice," I mumbled.

"You've ruined my good mood."

I raised my eyebrow. "You, in a good mood? I live to see the day..."

She didn't reply but the scowl on her face deepened and I decided not to push it. I tried my best not to touch her as I climbed the metal steps, but as I ascended I heard her say something under her breath.

"What was that?"

"I said it'll be your fault if she gets hurt again!" she shouted, composure completely shattered. She stared at me with bared teeth and a glare that would have made even a man completely clad in knight's armor falter.

"Who? Lucy?"

Why would she get hurt?

"Shut up!" she shouted, and clumsily fiddled with the window lock. I watched for a few seconds as she failed to unlock the latch, cursing, so I knelt down beside her and with a flick of my thumb opened the mechanism. "I don't need your help!" she spat as she threw open the window and climbed through, just to escape me.

She was probably just making some off-hand comment I wasn't supposed to hear, I thought, pushing any questions to the back of my mind.

"Took your sweet time!" Nina yelled, waving at me from across the rooftop. She was sitting in front of the bench and Apronas was behind her, a stern face of concentration focused on braiding my friend's hair. "Your lunch is in my bag, just go ahead and grab it," she said, so I did, although I was quite wary of digging through a girls' bookbag. Personal hygiene products and all. I pushed past her books and old candy wrappers until I found the lunch box, and as I pulled it out I accidentally bumped her phone and it fell out.

"Oh, crap! Sorry Nina!" I cried, quickly picking it up and flipping it open to see if it was broken. The screen flashed to life, revealing no damage but a message... from Miyamoto.

I felt a shadow fall across my face.

"Here, you've got a text," I muttered, handing her the phone.

"Thanks!" she gleefully replied.

"*I can't wait to see you tonight*," Apronas read aloud, imitating a boy's voice. "Ooh Nina, are you going dating tonight?" She laughed, raising an eyebrow at me. Trying to gauge my reaction I guess. Nina tried to turn but Apronas's fingers were so tightly wound in her hair and she hissed in pain, realizing that she was trapped.

"It's not a *date*! We're going out with friends!" Nina exclaimed as she snapped her phone shut.

"*Oenos* and and I are going dating tonight, maybe we all do a double dating?" Apronas said and I choked on my sandwich.

"Firstly!" I coughed, beating on my chest with closed fists. "Don't call it a date, that's misleading! And secondly, that's not my name!"

"Well..." she said with a smile, a rather wicked one that made me break out in a cold sweat. "That is what *you* called it, no?"

I could feel the blood drain from my face, and dropping to my knees I protested heavily, trying desperately to explain myself to Nina who just crossed her arms and looked away.

Apronas laughed the whole time.

Eventually I gave up and walked over to the edge of the roof to look down at all the students below. Apronas was humming to herself and Nina was silent, but I heard something else. A violin. My ears strained to hear the mellow notes of the lightly caressed strings, and I followed the sound around the corner of the building. It was playing so softly, and so isolated from everyone else. Isn't the point of playing an instrument to be heard? Looking over the edge I saw a girl with copper hair playing the instrument alone and I shrank back instinctively.

She was learning violin?

What else had I missed?

Slowly I regained my confidence, but by the time I peered over again she was gone.

When the last bell of the day rang I found Lucy waiting for me outside in the hall, a large stack of books in her arms.

"What's up, Luce?"

"Would you like to come to dinner with me tonight?" she asked.

"What exactly do you mean?" I coughed in surprise.

I could see Tobey staring at me in shock from within the class's doors.

"A few of the girls invited me out to dinner tonight but I don't want to go alone, so I thought I'd ask if you wanted to tag along?"

I sighed, relieved. "Sure, I'll come. Just don't make it sound like a date next time, okay?"

Her face went red upon hearing that. "I did not, did I?"

"You did," Tobey interjected as he walked past.

"I did not!" she shouted, her voice small and her defiant expression cute. "I-in any case, could I catch your digits?"

Could she not hear herself?

Walking through the school gates I was eager to get home, flick the TV on and just relax, spending the evening watching Miss. Morina Winslow adverts, but upon seeing Apronas I remembered with a heavy heart the plans I'd made the previous night.

"I'll catch you later," I said to Tobey, giving him a glum wave goodbye. Apronas met me with a smile I couldn't decipher the intent of. We began walking down the hills towards the sea-front shops, but as she told me what she had planned for the afternoon I thought it all sounded a bit... *couple-y*. With any other girl I wouldn't have minded, but with her? No thanks.

"These look so... *arkita*!" she exclaimed with a tug of my shirt, dragging me to a summer-clothing store and pointing at the mannequins within. She pulled me inside and immediately began taking bikinis off of racks and holding to her waist or chest, asking my opinion. I tried to be modest, but she insisted I pick one I thought suited her best.

"What's the appeal of these things anyway?" I asked, pinching a fluorescent green abomination between my fingers. She had decided to go into the changing room to try some on so I was left talking to a cloth partition.

"What's an *appeal*? Isn't that a fruit?"

"Well, no. You're thinking of an apple."

"Of course!" she said with misplaced confidence.

What?

"What I mean is: why do you like these things?"

"Easy," she said, pulling back the curtain. Revealing her tan body, all toned curves and soft edges. She stepped closer to me, face to face. "I *love* looking my best. It makes boys like you squirm." She placed a hand on my chest. "And I can just tell your imaginations go wild." She'd been leaning in as she'd spoken, her voice getting softer and more soaked with... something. Her breath was sweet and I immediately felt self-conscious of mine. Then she stepped back and twirled, laughing as she allowed me to see her best angles. Of which there were many.

"Drooling yet?" she asked, looking over her shoulder so I could admire her... back.

"Hardly," I swallowed, "blue isn't your colour."

"Nonsense Oenos, you're just trying to make me take it off." She winked. "I'll try on another one then. Maybe you'll like purple?" she said, stepping back into the changing room.

I sighed and stepped outside for some fresh air.

"Heck of a girl you got yourself there," said a voice from behind me. A familiar face smiled at me from behind rectangular shades. It was a dude I knew as 'Money', one of my sister's friends. I'd forgotten he worked at an ice-cream shack. Heck, I'd forgotten he existed at all! "New lady-friend?"

I scowled. "Lady, yes. Friend, not so much. Girl's ego is bigger than her bust."

"That's hard to believe," he chuckled, and lowered his newspaper. "What're you doing with her? Weren't you fawning over some other girl?"

I'm not sure exactly what information my sister had fed to him. I could only hope that it wasn't grossly exaggerated. Then again he was running off two-year-old information.

"Who, Nina?"

"No, not her." He shook his head confused. "She had some other name. Real regal."

"I'm not sure." I said, sure.

"Eh whatever. So this is Nina then?"

I groaned internally.

"No, this is Nina's friend Apronas. She's a foreign transfer student."

"Right, right." He nodded, leaning back. "Girls are trouble, little man." He lowered his glasses and winked, tapping the side of his head. "Anyway, could you help me? I need to anagram the word popsicle."

"Why?"

He waved the newspaper at me.

"Oh right. Polices?"

"Oh that's good." He said, scribbling.

"Copies?"

"I have that one."

"What do you have already?"

He squinted as he read his list. "I've got copies, polices, scope, pipes..."

"Oh, how about 'pops I scle'?" I suggested, and he gave me a strange look that I could understand even from behind his glasses. He was wondering why I wasn't in the loony bin. "What? It's the best I've got." I shrugged, and from within the store I heard Apronas's call.

Begrudgingly I went in, waving goodbye to Money and immediately blushing upon seeing Apronas wearing one heck of an outfit. It fit her in all the right places and accentuated her in others, but it was definitely something you wouldn't have your girlfriend wear within a mile of your parents. Heck, it looked like something you'd only wear privately!

"This must be the one, no?" she giggled upon seeing my reaction.

"Y-yeah... I think so," I said, admiring the ceiling and scratching the back of my head.

"Perfect! I shall return," she said, sauntering back into the changing rooms. A minute later she came back in her school uniform and dumped a pile of clothing on the counter, grabbing a pair of display glasses on and proclaiming: "He'll pay."

Before I could argue or bring up a single point of contention she left, and the glare the clerk gave me said: '*I'm not putting this back if you can't pay.*' And let me tell you, my wallet was a lot lighter after I left the store.

"Free ice-cream for the cute couple!" Money declared with a large smile, and Apronas giggled. I tried to refuse but my foreign companion gladly accepted the offer, even choosing the flavour of my scoop.

How dictatorial.

As she handed me my cone I noticed Money give me a grin and a thumbs up, mouthing the words 'good luck,' as I shook my head. We continued our walk down the pier while I struggled with the weight of Apronas's shopping bags.

"Oops," she said, and I turned my head to see that some of her ice cream had melted and dripped onto her shirt. Seeing me look her way she swifty undid her top button, laughing softly as she did so. "I can't let it stain my shirt now, can I?" Her voice was sultry and raspy, like something from a movie.

No, not a movie. Not a high-budget one anyway.

I looked away with a blush.

The rest of the afternoon passed much the same way. We'd enter a store, she'd try on something revealing, I'd get flustered and we'd leave. It was quite tiring in all honesty. I thanked the Goddesses above that time hadn't paused during the trip, otherwise I'd have thrown myself into the bay. After exiting the final store on the pier she stretched, and cricked her neck.

"What should I wear for our double date with Nina?" she said with a nasty smile. "What would she hate?"

She was no doubt hoping for my pitiful cooperation, but relief and hope had grown in my chest upon seeing the time on my watch. "Sorry, I already have plans!" I declared with a cheer.

And ran away.

Chapter Five
"Oh, you're here too."

On the way home I had a quick text-exchange with Lucy as we set up our plans for dinner, which were roughly to get dressed and be at the restaurant around seven, stopping by her place to pick her up on the way over. I was surprised to find out that she lived in a really nice part of town. What I guess you could call the 'suburbs'. Her parents were overly friendly, shaking my hand and inviting me over for dinner some time, smiling the whole way. Lucy and her mom looked like a mirror of one another. You could even mistake her mother for being her older sister.

Lucy's parents stood on the front porch and waved energetically as we left, telling us to have a great time. I teased her about it of course, but she didn't have to suffer for long as we arrived at the restaurant sooner than expected. It was a classy joint in the centre of the New Business District and was nowhere I'd have gone on my own, both due to the sophisticated atmosphere and the outrageous prices.

Her friends waved us over as we entered, beckoning us to a large glossy wooden table surrounded by hanging lights. They handed us a menu as we sat, and greeted her with a cheer. Among them was Nina, and when she saw me with Lucy her face fell to something resembling a scowl. "Oh. You're here too," she said bluntly.

No need to be considerate of my feelings, I guess.

A "Howdy!" came with an outstretched hand which I instinctively shook before realizing that it belonged to Miyamoto. Who was sitting beside Nina.

Oh. You're here too.

I quickly browsed through the menu, searching for the cheapest thing to order, and when the waitress asked what we wanted to drink

I ended up asking for water. The rest of the group had ordered extravagant coffee blends and sipped at them whilst commenting on their refined aromas.

I definitely felt like a fish out of water.

"Nina's told me a lot about you," said Miyamoto, and I tore my eyes away from the metal chandelier to look at his goofy face. "Is it true that you were on the track team?"

I groaned internally. Of course she had told him about that. It was my only accolade, and the only thing of worth I had ever achieved. "I was." Once. I was good at it too, even setting a few records.

"Do you have any tips? I've been thinking of joining the track team myself." He said with an earnest smile on his face, one I soon began imagining doing bad things to. I suspected his wanting to join the team had something to do with Nina being on it.

"Yeah, don't try too hard!" I laughed, "but no, really. Try to land on the front of your foot, not your heel. It's bad for your bones."

"Wow, thanks!" he said and sat back, nodding. Repeating my words to himself. I didn't know I was such a vassal of wisdom, but every word I said he ate up. Taking it as absolute truth. I don't know why, exactly. Maybe he was trying to impress me. Eventually he asked the one question I'd been dreading. "So why did you stop running?"

A baseball bat.

"I got tired of it, plain and simple," I lied with a smile.

Throughout the rest of the meal time had only paused once, and not even for very long. I thought it was rather fortunate. Miyamoto and Suzu dragged me into a conversation about our favourite actresses, and everyone gave me strange looks when I was only able to list off b-list actresses from various TV dramas. Nina didn't look too impressed with me either.

But then the conversation turned dark, with Leon (unimportant, don't even bother remembering him) leaning in and speaking with a low tone. "What do you guys think of the slashings?" he said.

Everyone began whispering then, each person exchanging their thoughts and opinions on what exactly had been going on. "Someone was stabbed in the north end yesterday!"

"Oh my... who?"

"Some businessman, he got sent to the hospital in critical condition."

"Oh, I heard about this on the news this morning!" A girl added. "There were no witnesses who saw the slasher, right?"

"Exactly right!" Suzu interjected, her face so close to the candles on the table I was sure she was millimetres away from being set alight. "It's been getting worse, it happened the day before too."

"Really, where?" Nina asked, leaning on one elbow.

"In the alleyways off the main street."

I felt a pressure around my leg, and looking down I saw Lucy's hand gripping my knee.

"He didn't see anybody either, did he?"

"No..."

"We seem to have a blade in the dark..." Leon whispered, looking at each of our faces for dramatic effect. "They're lurking around dark alleyways, attacking innocent bystanders... any one of us could be next!" He then gave his best impression of a cheesy vampire villain laugh. All he was missing was perfectly timed lightning.

"Stop it, Leon!"

"You're too much!"

And: "Eek!" Were some of the various responses.

I rolled my eyes, but Lucy was completely horrified, staring at Leon with her eyes and mouth forming three perfect circles. She turned to me with the same expression and I almost laughed. "We were on the main street just two days ago!" she exclaimed, "it could have been us!"

"Somehow I doubt that," I said, "also, do you mind?"

She looked down and pulled her hand away with a blush. With that dealt with I relaxed, and looking across the table I found Nina staring at me. She didn't pull her gaze away so neither did I. The group kept talking and exchanging theories, and the vendor outside called for someone to buy his newspapers as the waitress asked for someone's order, but they were all silent to me. Time hadn't paused, but our eyes remained locked. She flicked her eyes over to Lucy and raised an eyebrow.

I wasn't sure what she was asking so I raised my eyebrow in return.

She lightly shook her head.

I didn't know what to do so I nodded.

The expression on her face looked reminiscent of someone whose favourite pencil's lead had just snapped, and she turned away from me with a huff, joining in with the conversation. The topic had changed from murder mysteries, to horror movies, then regular movies, and then whether or not the book was better than the movie. I couldn't say I knew which book or movie they were talking about. During a lull in the conversation my attention slipped away and I ended up staring out the window.

Among the everyday passerby I saw a cat as black as the night, or really, I just saw its silhouette as it strutted down the street. That wasn't odd in itself. A little while later I saw Tobey covered from head-to-toe in clumpy, sodden mud, on his hands and knees, ducking from alleyway to alleyway, following the cat with a determined look on his face. I stared, confounded and confused as he glanced over his shoulder and rushed hunched over to the next alley. Now *that* was odd. A little while later I saw a calico cat calmly strolling down the lane behind him.

Just what kind of beef had he gotten into with the felines?

After that was dessert which I tried to opt out of but Lucy, wanting to thank me for coming, decided to share a banana boat with me. As she fed me with a spoon I noticed Nina shaking, and her eye twitching, and she then grabbed Miyamoto and force fed him a parfait which he choked on.

As the hours wore on the group began to slowly disband, leaving in twos and threes, until Lucy eventually placed a hand on my shoulder and smiled. "Hey O-ey," she had said. "Is it okay if I go to Lulu's house to watch a movie?"

Why was she asking me?

"Uh, sure? You don't need to ask," I chuckled weakly. "It's perfectly fine. Do whatever you like, it's your night." I gave her an awkward smile and she hugged me.

"Thank you," she replied with an awkward smile of her own. "I'll see you later, goodnight!" She waved, and I waved back as she left with a group of her friends. Their chatter was excited and I could hear them giggling happily even from a street away.

Nina was staring at me.

What should I do?

What should I say?

Prepare for emergency evacuation sequence in 3...2...1...

"Well." I slapped my knees and stood up. "It's about time I head home. Thanks for the evening, guys." I gave a stiff wave to those still remaining, and Nina's stare didn't waver as she raised a hand.

"See you," she said coldly.

I made my way to the counter but they had told me that Lucy had paid my bill. I groaned upon hearing this. That girl... She didn't have to. I'll have to pay her back, I thought as I hurried out of the cafe and into the night, trying to ignore Nina's prodding eyes glaring through the shop window.

The cool air and the moon kept me company on my odyssey, although I found myself thinking of the days I used to run, reminded of the freedom by Miyamoto's incessant questioning. Reminded of the orange dirt tracks and the thin painted lines. The wind on my face, the sweat coating my body with a glorious sheen, the heaving for air after breaking the ribbon. Feeling like I could run forever.

Chapter Six

"Not a man, nor an Entity."

I woke up late the next day, around noon. The TV was still on from last night and was now broadcasting some live concert for children where cartoon mascots played the instruments. The big pink cat thing on the drums was going wild. From where I lay the sun shone directly into my eyes, and was the only reason I'd woken up at all. After flipping my phone open I discovered that the inbox was empty, and Nina also hadn't burst through the front door ordering me to put my tracksuit on so I could join her on a jog around town, so I stretched, glad that my weekend was already off to a good start.

I flipped the channel over to the infomercials and watched Miss. Morina Winslow as she described the prestige of some antique-style kitchenware that had just come into stock. Upon seeing a retro-style tea set that came with cups and a teapot I considered calling the number on-screen. I had even reached for the land-line but stopped myself upon seeing the price tag. Maybe I'd get it next century when I'd saved up enough.

After my muscles began to cramp I got up and stretched, stepping out onto the balcony for some fresh air. Far down below, the beach was absolutely packed. Even more so than usual. I guess people were as happy as I was about the good weather.

I called Tobey.

"Yo?" he answered on the first ring, as he always did. I could hear loud thuds and grunting on his end of the line.

"Yo," I replied, "weather's good, folks're on the beach. You wanna come over?"

"Yeah, sure man. I'll leave my sumo-wrestling practice on the double," he said, then hung up before I could even voice a question. I held my phone up and raised an eyebrow then heard a knock at the door.

Who could that be now?

Tobey, apparently. With a beach chair under one arm and a cooler box under the other.

His practice must have been in the neighborhood, I reasoned.

"What are you wearing?"

"What?" he said, looking down. "It's my uniform."

"It looks like a diaper."

"That's rude."

"Put some clothes on," I said, shaking my head as he waddled in with not much more than a roll of cloth between his unmentionables and I. If he were a larger gentleman he would have fit the role, but being as skinny as he was he'd never fit the bill. Since when did he do sumo anyway? After he got dressed we set ourselves up on the balcony with our beach chairs and soon everything was ready. We were each equipped with a compass, a telescope, and a notebook, and we sat for hours spying on the people below, sipping on our medley of beverages which sat within the cooler.

"Ooh, tango with a pink bikini at 108," he'd report.

"Sighting confirmed," I'd reply, "requesting an estimation of measurements."

"On it."

...

"Total wipeout at 62!" I cried, mentioning his utter lack of board control in my notebook.

"He's gonna feel that in the morning," Tobey added.

"I'm just hoping he stays away from everyone else or there'll be a burial."

...

"I-is that...?" Tobey muttered excitedly, shifting the telescope and adjusting the dials. "Is that Apronas at 90?"

I angled my lens, and as she turned around Tobey and I looked at eachother.

"Dear Goddesses... I hope not," he said.

"No, she doesn't look like that in a bikini at at all."

He tilted his head. "What do you mean?"

"She looks way better in one than that... thing."

"When did you see her in a bikini? Wait, you saw her in a bikini?" Tobey leaped up and grabbed my collar, shaking me violently. "Tell me everything, now!"

...

"Warning, beached whale at 165," I said.

Tobey looked at me. "Dude, rude."

"No really, look!" I said, this time pointing at the blob in the distance.

"Oh damn. You're right."

...

"Yo, shark fin at 46." Tobey noted, then he looked up at me as we realized.

"Shark!?"

When the sun had finally set but the light hadn't fully faded Tobey suggested that we head into town to grab some dinner. I agreed as long as he'd pick up the tab, and so we packed up our people-watching kit and strolled down the roads that winded their way into the Old Business District. All the best food joints were there. Genuine family-recipes and heartfelt meals were cooked and crafted by older folks who were keeping the culture and heart of our town alive. Upon seeing neon signs and wooden blocks advertising noodle bars we knew we were in the right place.

"A grizzly bear could *not* beat a group of honey badgers," I protested.

"How can you be so sure?" Tobey chided, "Have you run the simulations?"

"No, but I know the soul of a honey badger is undefeatable."

"Ah..." Tobey rubbed his chin. "I didn't account for that."

"Exactly," I said, eyes closed and confident. "A *single* honey badger could beat a bear, if it wanted to."

"Alright, but I'm not so sure o–"

"Hey guys!" A roaring voice came, interrupting all thought. Accompanying it was a log of muscle which wrapped itself around our heads and locked us in a hug, shaking us violently. "Where're you two off to?"

I tapped at the behemoth's arm and gasped for air. Tobey was doing the same. "F-food, food!" I choked and we were released, followed by a slap on the back.

"I'm up for food!" David cheered, "I'm parched!"

"You mean starved, right?" Tobey coughed.

"Eh, same turd different smell."

I don't think that's how that saying goes.

"Where'd you come from?" I grunted, rubbing my back.

"Practice."

Explains the smell.

"Athletics Celebration Day is coming up soon and Coach wants us all to be on our A game so we can shame all you weaklings with our superior physical prowesses." He grinned at me. "You know how it is."

I placed a hand on David's boulder-shaped shoulder. "You're impressive enough, bro."

"Thanks!" He gave me a thumbs up. "Now what're we eatin'?"

"I whittled the choices down to burgers or steak, but this guy's horribly indecisive" Tobey said, throwing a thumb my way. "Which one are you partial to?"

"Out of those two? Neither. Follow me boys, I know a damn good place."

With that, David charged on valiantly and though Tobey and I exchanged a glance we followed him anyway, ducking down a side alley and across a park, then down near the pier and turning back on ourselves. I thought for sure he had gotten lost a moment before he proclaimed we'd arrived, standing with his arms wide open praising a hole-in-the-wall joint.

"This is your suggestion? A stay-drink place?" I queried, a little unimpressed.

"Yeah man! Mr. Kobayashi has the best noodles in town, hands down."

"Are we even old enough to enter?" Tobey asked and David slapped his back so hard I thought I could hear his spine snap.

"Don't worry glasses-man, it ain't a bar so as long as we don't order alcohol there shouldn't be a problem. C'mon, follow me," David said, ducking through the front door and into a dimly-lit yet cozy little space decorated with millions of posters and advertisements for a city on the other side of the country. I'm sure all the posters were made long before my birth, and the postcards and pictures on the walls of patrons definitely were. The roof was low but the room was wide, with a bar counter full of people and tables crowding the space. In the corner was a stage with a man singing. Well, it was less singing and something more closely related to the moaning you'd hear from a dying elk. David edged his way past customers who all knew him by name and waved Mr. Kobayashi down, calling his name and receiving an excited wave in return. The two shook hands and chatted about their day. I nudged Tobey with my elbow.

"*Is it just me, or has the guy singing not blinked yet?*" I whispered.

"*No, you're right. He hasn't. And he's been staring at us the whole time.*"

"*Why's he singing Christmas songs? It's the middle of summer.*"

"*I don't know, and I'm too scared to ask.*"

"Yo boys!" David called out, saving us from the staring eyes of the Moaning Christmas Man and waving us over to a table in the corner by the door. We joined him and sat down, opening up a menu to peruse the contents.

"What should we order?" I asked.

"I got that covered," David said with a grin.

"You didn't get us anything funny did you?"

He shook his head. "Trust me bro. So uh, what do you guys think of the rumours everybody's on about?"

I groaned.

"The teleporter, the slasher, or the sewer dolphin man?" Tobey asked, and David looked at me with a worrisome expression.

"The... the first two."

"Give it a rest," I sighed, "I swear this is all I hear about. There's no teleporter, and the slasher is just some random dude. Probably Oscar. There's a million reasons as to why he hasn't been caught, and I'm tired of talking about it."

"Why are you so against the idea of teleporters?" Tobey asked coyly.

"Because it's stupid, that's why. There's a nonzero chance that there's one, let alone two teleporters in this town." I reasoned that teleporters were far different than Time Pausers. "And the only reason the slasher is still out there is because of police negligence. Or lack of witnesses."

"What do you think about aliens?" David put forward.

"What do aliens have to do with anything?" I snapped.

"I was just curious, damn," he mumbled.

"I guess I believe in them, but chances that they're on Earth is close to nil."

Tobey nodded. "Statistically a-" he raised two fingers and air quoted, rolling his eyes, "-'teleporter' living here is improbable, and the chances that an alien is here too is astoundingly low. Realistically it's impossible but I do in fact believe they exist. No, it would be more accurate to say I *know* they exist."

"Oh really? How can you be so sure?"

"Because I am one." He poked his tongue out.

Mr. Kobayashi, the master of the Stay-Drink place, came over with pure bowls balanced expertly on his outstretched arms and deftly he swung them onto the table. The steaming brothy hand-pulled noodles drenched my aching nose in an aroma that was an absolute treat to the senses. I could instantly see why David ordered this.

"Thanks for the food!" We all cheered and Mr. Kobayashi gave us a wink.

I grabbed my chopsticks and pulled the noodles from the broth, delighting in the view of the bubbly liquid dripping onto the meat below. I blew softly to cool it down but David scoffed his meal with eyes full of tears and dramatic exhales of fiery breath.

"What do you guys think of Apronas?" Tobey posed quite suddenly and breaking the silence, dipping his chopsticks in his broth.

"Who's that?" David asked, gulping down a string of noodle.

"She's the transfer student, you haven't heard of her?"

"No, I know now. I'm guessing she was that tanned chick everyone's been crowding around the last few days."

"That's the one," Tobey confirmed, then looked at me. "So?"

"Eh," I shrugged, "she's not hard on the eyes, but the annoying part is that she knows it. Girl has no boundaries either."

"What about Nina?"

I coughed up a noodle. "What about Nina?"

He raised an eyebrow and gave a smile I wanted to punch. "I'm just asking what you think of her, that's all."

"Well slow your roll, cowboy. You haven't told us what *you* think of Apronas yet."

Tobey leaned back and cupped his chin, giving his response some serious thought. "I think she's very... interesting."

"Is that all? Really?"

Tobey began fiddling with his chopsticks. "There's something about her that I know I know, but that I can't recall, no matter how much I try. I keep asking her but she won't admit it." He sipped on a noodle. "Nina?"

My next move was desperate, and I knew that all I was doing was stalling for time, but I played my trap card.

"Bother David, I'm trying to eat!"

"Huh?" he replied, looking at the two of us. "I don't even know what she looks like."

"No, not her," I said, punching his arm. "Keep up!"

"Eileen, what do you think of her?" Tobey added.

David's face went beet red in a flash. "She's nice."

I looked at Tobey. He Looked at me. The Moaning Christmas Man stared at us.

Tobey elbowed David in the ribs with a grin. "You think she's *nice,* eh?"

"That's what I said, now leave me alone!" He hunkered over his bowl.

"Nice on the eyes? Nice on the ears? Nice to imagine kissing?" I puckering my lips and fluttered my eyelashes. David slammed his hands on the table.

"Shut it you two! You're disrespecting a proper lady! Eileen is no two-bit dame, she's the cream of the crop, alright?" He closed his eyes and raised a finger. I had the same habit when declaring something with passion, so I knew he was serious. "She's incredibly intelligent, with a mind so expansive and calm I'm sure the Goddess Ruina based heaven off of it. And don't even get me started on her hair and the honeyed silk that it is, like a waterfall of gentle care and tender beauty. Or her perfume... ah, strawberries..." David's cheeks turned pink and his mind went to a place far away, and he began sighing and mumbling to himself.

Tobey turned to me. "Your turn."

I sighed. How to condense Nina down to one sentence? It couldn't be done. It would be a disservice to her, plain and simple. I'd known her for around three years now, and I saw her so often I never really had the time to think about it. I know I act a fool, but I really appreciated everything she did for me. Even just being around was enough to make my face hurt from smiling so much. She'd been there after Oscar and... *her*. She was there for me after the doctor told me I wouldn't be able to run again. She'd been by my side the whole time. An ever-shining light in the ever-worsening state of my life. I just wish I could somehow repay her for beaming that worry-dashing smile my way every day.

"She's nice."

Chapter Seven
"Lowlife, lowlife."

Sunday started much like Saturday, with me waking up on the couch and Miss. Morina Winslow singing the praises of a self-drying towel. The unending gaze of the Moaning Christmas Man had invaded my dreams, but the dinner David had treated us to was well worth the nightmares. I had to give him credit. Tobey had walked me home just to tell me that my milk was out of date. Far past it actually.

"You could probably turn it into yogurt at this point," he'd said.

Accompanying the recollection of last night's events was the grumbling of my unfed stomach. My kitchen truly was devoid of anything edible so I made myself a list, checked the coupons in the weekly flyers, and made my way downtown. The shopping list ended up being as long as my arm after I checked the contents of the fridge and pantry but I remained strong and marched forward. My shopping trip was rather delightful despite my grumbling; with birds singing and the sun shining and married couples going to the park with their kids and their dogs. The warmth of the day extended to the elderly shop-keepers who smiled as I entered and gave me discounts for being 'such a nice young man'. It wasn't long before I found myself on the return trip, in high spirits and saddled with bags full of groceries. I was in such a good mood that I decided to take the scenic route home through the winding uphill roads of the Old Town. There were no connecting roads, but I knew of a few little walkways that ducked beneath the shade of massive trees, with little bridges over shining creeks that let you see the koi swimming within. It was not uncommon for little kids to wade in knee-deep and try to catch the fish with their bare hands.

Akera was thrown to the floor by some guy with tattoo sleeves. There was a group surrounding him, all similarly dressed with popped collars and a lack of ties. No one tried to stop him as he grabbed her by the hair and yanked, causing her to scream.

"Hey!" I yelled, immediately regretting my decision as the group turned to face me with a sneer.

"What?" The guy pulling her hair spoke with such a casual tone that I was caught off-guard. He made it sound like I'd interrupted his breakfast or something.

"You uh, shouldn't do that. To her, I mean," I stuttered lamely. The man let go of her hair and she dropped with a thud, scraping her hands on the warm tarmac. With exaggerated swagger he approached me.

"Looks like her knight in shining armor has appeared," he said and the group chuckled. The man came to a stop so awfully close that I shrunk back half a step. He wasn't as big as David, and he was only half as menacing as Oscar, but there was just something more intimidating about an adult threatening you. He stooped forward and looked into my eyes, grinning. "Why are you telling me to stop?"

What kind of stupid question is that?

"Because... it's bad to hurt people?"

I sighed internally. This was not going well.

"Didja stop to think that maybe she deserves it?" he hissed at me, his smile gone. I looked over his shoulder and saw Akera staring back. Her unkempt hair hung over eyes that burned with a raging fire. I thought she was about to go ballistic and tear him apart like a beast, but she made no effort to get up. "You look rather roughed up yourself, boy. Tell me, are you a fighter?" he continued, placing a hand on my shoulder and squeezing so hard I twisted in pain.

I shook my head.

"Ah, that's disappointing," he tutted, shaking his head and looking at me as if I were some pathetic twerp. Which is exactly what I am. "I was gonna ask if you wanted to take her place."

"Leave him alone, Dan. He's even more of a coward than you."

"Oh, you two know each other?" His grin returned. "Even when you try to help her she insults you. But she's just like that, I'm sure you know." He sent a punch into my stomach that caused me to double over and drop my groceries. One of the bags split open and vegetables rolled across the road just as he threw another punch that caused my chest to squeeze all the air out of me. I dropped to my knees gasping.

"She wasn't lying," he muttered in disgust, and stood on a plump red tomato I had been looking forward to eating. As I coughed I felt myself start to decay, my edges lose definition. A static buzz blurred my features and warped my silhouette as I gripped the ground and felt the road give way to my fingers. My fists were full of rubble. An eye opened in the centre of my forehead, slowly awakening after a long, long slumber. All my rage bubbled up and spilled over, hissing as it hit the ground. My body trembled.

I took a breath. I returned.

Dan strolled over to Akera and raised her chin with a finger. "You have until next Sunday, that's *it*." He gripped her face, holding it tight and jerking her head up. "If I don't have my money by then I'm going to break every bone in your body..." He leaned in, face dark. "And I'll enjoy it, too."

Then he and his crew strolled off, walking past me and down into town. I thought that one of them were going to send a kick into my ribs, or punch my head, or something, but they just spoke of yesterdays 'game', their voices casual. Ignoring me and laughing. I guess that I was unimportant. A piece of discarded trash.

Akera was fighting with herself, too. Resisting the urge to throw one last insult at him. I coughed and got to one knee.

"What did you do to piss *Dan* off?" I asked. I began to pick up my scattered groceries while she stood straight and dusted herself off, reaching into her jacket for a pack of cigarettes and a lighter. I could see her thinking as she lit one, deciding how much to tell me. Eventually she sighed.

"I owe him. Big time." She clenched her jaw and shook her head. "I was supposed to deliver something for him but I got cold feet and the police found it."

"What are you going to do?"

She shrugged. "I'll think of something."

Akera placed the cigarette in my mouth and we stood for a bit in silence. The atmosphere was too awkward for me to handle.

"Hungry?"

"Get lost," she scowled and stormed away.

I sighed and picked up my leeks.

Chapter Eight
"Average Joe Blues."

The next day I woke up earlier than usual. Two hours earlier in fact. I reasoned that my Time-Pausing compatriots had something to do with it, but for once I didn't mind. I got myself all nice and ready for the day, even taking the time to iron my shirt during the morning commercials, prepare some lunch, and do a little bit of cleaning.

The look of surprise upon Nina's face as she walked up the hill to find me waiting there for her was priceless, and with a befuddled expression she asked me "Are you feeling okay?"

"Better than ever!" I declared, "I got up early today and I feel grand!"

"Something is definitely wrong, what happened?" she asked, tilting her head and stepping forward.

"No, nothing happened," I laughed, "time just must've paused while I was sleeping. That's why I'm up right now."

Her expression changed then, and she shook her head. "So it's not through any effort of your own that you're here right now?"

I stuck my tongue out at her and she stuck hers out at me.

The walk to school that day was a completely different experience. I got to see what it was like to be an average Joe getting to school at the average time. The birds sang a different song and the air was crisper. Nina wasn't in such a good mood though, and it only worsened when we chanced upon Apronas along the way.

"Good morning Nina~" Apronas sang like a bluebird, "and good morning to you, *Oenos*." She linked her arm through mine and pulled me close, grinning at Nina.

"Morning," Nina scowled.

"How was your weekends?" Apronas asked, "Have fun?"

"Lots of it," Nina said through gritted teeth. Her bad mood was palpable, radiating off of her like evaporating water.

"So many boys talked with me at the beach yesterday. They couldn't keep their eyes away from myself!" Apronas ran her fingers through her hair then squeezed my arm. "But none of them were as handsome as *you*."

Nina spun on her heel and pointed a finger at Apronas. I watched as the vein in the centre of her forehead bulged and her eye twitch, but Apronas had nothing but a wicked smile to give in return.

"You..." Nina's voice was gravel. "You should..." Then she looked at me and sighed. "You should join us for lunch," she said, defeated, and turned away.

What was up with her?

Apronas giggled then let go of my arm and began skipping alongside us. "I would love to!" she sang.

Tobey's spectacled face and pointed hair appeared over the crest of the hill and I waved at him. Upon seeing me he looked at his watch, face quizzical. Then he looked up at the sky.

"What's up?"

"I just thought I'd never see the day *you* were early. I'm trying to see if the sky's about to fall down or something."

"Ha, ha. Very funny. I can be reliable."

"Mmhmm." He nodded. "Rarely."

"That's a lot more than you are!"

"Apronas," he said, turning away from me and sidling next to her. "How was the beach?"

Apronas raised an eyebrow. "You have been following me?"

"W-well no," he stammered, "I was selling ice-cream at the beach and I just so happened to see you walk by, you know. And I thought I should say 'hi' so I began walking behind you, but then so many people began talking to you, and I thought it would be rude to interrupt so I didn't say anything and by the time I thought I should leave we'd already been on the beach for half an hour. But then I thought 'I've already been here for however long, I might as well say hi' so I approached you, but then you put those sunglasses on and lay down so I stood above you for a while trying to get your attention."

"You work at an ice-cream store?"

"Er, uh, no..." he admitted sheepishly.

I shook my head as Apronas started accusing him of this, that, and the other, and Tobey failed dramatically to defend himself. He just kept digging the hole deeper and deeper. The language barrier proved to be of no help in the situation as she started yelling at him in her mother tongue, slapping him on the back of the head as he tried to explain 'no, he hadn't been creepy. He'd been gentlemanly.'

Nina was lagging behind, scowling again. Her gaze was directed to the floor and she was muttering under her breath. I tapped her hand and she looked at me, forest floor eyes. Oh. What should I say?

"Do anything interesting on the weekend?"

"I had a driver's test but I failed it. My instructor was practically praying that we'd make it back to the office alive, and I even got pulled over by a policeman twice."

Ah, maybe that was the reason for her bad mood.

"My little sister also had a chess game, which she won. She did something called a 'Fiddlewin and Bunglehole gambit' in the last five minutes and everybody cheered." She pinched the bridge of her nose. "I still don't even know what that means."

"Don't worry, neither do." I smiled.

"Yeah, but that's to be expected."

Ouch.

"Those two are getting along like a house on fire," I said, pointing at Tobey and Apronas. It seemed like the hole he'd dug was big enough to fit a whale, seeing as how she was threatening to call the police and they were wrestling over her phone.

"Yeah. It's good to see her making friends..." Nina's tone was strained.

"It sounds like there's a 'but' there."

"But nothing! She's *super* fun to be around," she snapped, staring at me with the world record for tightest smile. "And speaking of houses on fire, you and *her* seem to be getting close."

"Who, Apronas?"

"Her too!"

"What do you mean 'too'?"

Her eye began twitching. She was seriously mad that I wasn't getting it. "I'm talking about Lucy. You're pretty much following her around like a dog on a leash! She's bad news."

"What makes you say that?"

"Her choice in boys for one," she sneered, then began counting on her fingers. "Smoking, drinking, ditching class. Drugs too, probably. Both her and Akera are bad news."

"Are you forgetting that I'm just like them?"

She choked on her words.

"You're not... you're. Reformed." Her anger dissipated and she looked at me like a deflated balloon. I gave her a gentle smile and put my arm around her shoulder.

"I don't know why you're getting so mad. I'm still *your* gopher."

"So you're my gopher now? Even though I'm the one who makes you lunch, and gets you up, and forces you to go outside, and who helps you study..."

"Yeah, yeah, yeah, I get the point. But today is different."

I patted my book bag and flashed a grin. "Today I'm treating *you* to lunch."

"Let's hope I survive the food poisoning," she said, her good natured smile having returned.

The school building and the slowly undressing oak trees out front began peeking over the top of the next hill, and it felt odd arriving without the bell telling me to hurry up. The four of us split apart to put on our shoes, and for once I was the first one done. I leaned on Nina's locker door to watch her struggle to undo the double knot in her laces.

"Here, let me do that for you," I said, dropping to one knee.

"N-no, wait," she stuttered, but I ignored her and tugged at her laces. Her mind must have been miles away when she'd put her shoes on this morning as it was quite an effort getting it undone. A boy scout would have been proud of the knot she'd tied.

"Here, give me your foot," I said, and she followed suit. She had white socks on, clean and soft. I slipped the shoe around her foot and tugged at the laces.

"Are you busy tonight?" I asked, looking up at her. She looked away, cheeks red.

What was up with her?

"No. I'm not busy. Why?"

"Other foot," I said, distracted. "I was thinking of cooking dinner tonight. Wanna have another meal on me?"

"D-depends on what you're gonna make."

"How does spaghetti sound?" I stood and smiled at her but she was looking elsewhere. Behind her Tobey, Apronas, and David, stared at me with their mouths wide open.

"What?"

"Oh, uh, nothing," Tobey gulped, "See you in class!"

"What he said!" David nodded and rushed to follow.

"Enjoy your meal," Apronas said with a wink.

What was up with them? I looked back at Nina and she was finally returning my gaze. Slowly she rested her head on top of her locker door and looked down at me, forest floor eyes in soft summer shade. The cool sunlight and lack of students made this moment a quiet one. I could have sat there forever. She sighed. "Okay."

"Great." I got to my feet and shared a smile with her. "I'll see you later."

Waving goodbye I made my way to class, enjoying the lack of swarming students impeding my progress. I sat at my desk and pulled my books out before spending the next few minutes with my head resting on my hands and watching the world outside the window. When the bell finally rang and Mr. Washy stepped into the classroom we bowed, and for the first time in a long time I paid attention.

Very quickly did I realize exactly how far behind I was.

As I sat down across from Eileen she looked up and gave me a smile like a tulip in bloom. "Your face is looking better."

"You lie," I said, smiling. "Where's David?"

"I'm not sure," she replied, peeking over my shoulder. She seemed almost agitated. On edge. Nervous, maybe.

"What are we studying today?

"Sorry?" She gave me an incredulous look. "Study?"

"Yep," Tobey said, patting my shoulder as he arrived. "You're looking at a new man. O-boy here has turned a new leaf in life. He's responsible now."

"That I am." I affirmed with a nod.

"Okay, uh..." Eileen flicked through her textbook. "How good are you with mensuration?"

"You mean that thing girls do? Is that what we're studying in biology?" I asked.

Eileen's face went red. "No, it's uh, maths."

"Women mensurate in maths?"

Tobey slapped the back of my head. "You idiot, women can do that anywhere."

"I feel like you're missing the point here–" Eileen started, but then her face lit up and she waved. The smile she gave me was like a raindrop next to an ocean compared to the smile she gave David. "Over here!"

"Shhhh!" hissed the elderly librarian. She went ignored.

David took his seat next to Eileen, his attention immediately on me.

"This morning, did you really? You were serious?"

"Uh, yeah?" I was, wasn't I? Serious about what? When wasn't I serious?

David grinned. "Nice bro! I'm proud of you!"

I looked at Tobey for clarification but he was busy gyrating his head.

"Listen bro, my uncle works at the movie theatre in Old Town and he said they're doing early screenings for this movie that came out ten years ago or something-"

"-Oh, you mean that one about the postman?" Eileen asked, leaning forward.

"That's the one." David nodded. "How did you know?"

"I've seen the posters all over town, I love that movie! I've always wanted to see it again!"

David looked at me, swallowed, then turned to Eileen. "Well, um... Do you want to go? Tomorrow?" His face went red and he turned to me. "You should come too. You and Nina."

Aw sweet! Group outing! My luck today was impeccable!

"Sure man, that sounds great!" I said and gave him a high five. "You coming along, pardner?" I asked Tobey with some playful elbowing in tow. He looked confused and pointed at himself.

"Who, me?"

"Yeah man! Let's ask Apronas if she wants to come along!"

Tobey looked at David who sighed, and nodded. "Sure, why not."

"Splendid!" I said with a rather pleased grin, and flipped open my biology textbook. "So what page is mensuration on?"

The bell rang and I stretched. My brain had been completely worn out after an hour of intense use. "Good work team!" I said and gave a thumbs up to my crew.

"Sure thing." David returned my thumbs up.

"You really oughta study more..." Eileen said, shakily.

"No doubt. O-boy has a severe lack of braincells." Tobey nodded.

"Leave the kid alone!" David protested, "he's got more than enough muscle to make up for it!" He flexed his biceps and urged me to do the same. I laughed, but tensed my muscles and he gave me a look of approval. "See? He's got more guns than the military base."

"I know I wear glasses, but even *I* couldn't see anything," Tobey snickered.

"Maybe David needs specs too?" Eileen giggled.

"Oh whatever..." I muttered, pushing in my chair and shoving my books into my bag. As I swung it over my shoulder I flexed another bicep and grinned. "You two are just jealous!"

"Atta boy!" David cheered.

"I'll see you guys later." With a beaming grin I headed out the door.

"Yo man, I've got a reservation with the pottery teacher," Tobey said, rolling his neck and making it crick.

"Really? Why?"

"I watched that movie last night, you know, what's it called...? It's the one with the ghost?" He shook his hand dismissively. "Anyway, it got me really interested in clay sculptures so I called Ms. Linz and asked her to show me how to do it. She seemed really happy to teach me too."

"You have Ms. Linz's number?"

"I have everyone's number." He winked. "See you."

"Weirdo," I muttered and carried on, but I was stopped by a hand pinching at the loose cuff of my shirt. I came to find Eileen red faced and staring at her shoes right behind me.

"Oh hey, what's up?"

She clutched tightly at the stack of her books, but slowly she looked me in the eyes. "Can you please do me a favour?"

"No problem. What is it?" I asked and she retrieved a pink envelope from within a textbook. She paused for a moment before handing it to me. It had little drawings of flowers on it.

"Could you please put this in David's locker?"

"Sure. Did he forget this?" I asked and she looked into my eyes with a calculating gaze. It looked like she was trying to figure something out. She stared way too long.

"Yes," she finally nodded.

"Okay, you can count on me!" I declared and marched back over to the locker room. The air today was fresh, and carried tones of education and hope for the future. The sun poked between the branches of the inner courtyard's tree and I was thankful for every lick of warmth. Having slipped the letter through the opening of David's locker and patting the door as thanks, I came face to face with Oscar. He was glowering and hunched over. His foul mood the air bent around him and revealed a black, diseased aura. Not unlike Nina's this morning.

He threw his locker door open and tossed his shoes to the ground, kicking his own off and replacing them, all the while muttering and mumbling harsh words under his breath. I'd seen him like this a few times, and it never resulted in anything good. I would wager that he was getting bored. Standing up again he slammed the door shut and stepped forward, then stopped. He looked at me. The glare he directed at me was almost as bad as the Moaning Christmas Man's, but his eyes of blue fire hiding behind his black tendrils of hair definitely made it way, way worse.

"Your life doesn't matter," he started, "we're all just living in the aftermath of someone else's story."

He walked away.

I wondered what was bothering him.

I gave it no thought and tottered away, bouncing from one foot to the other, essentially skipping through the halls. I heard violin music in my heart and I dipped and danced, twirling like a professional ballet dancer up until I stepped wrong and pain shot up my right leg. I crashed to the floor and landed flat on my face.

"Hey stupid, are you okay?" Asked a voice that drew heavy on the vowels.

"I'm good!" I looked up with a smile. "Are you tomorrow afternoon?"

"What?"

"Sorry, free. I meant are you free tomorrow afternoon?"

"Why?"

"We're gonna go to the movies, I thought you might want to come?"

She stared at me and I clasped my hands together, pleading until eventually she rolled her eyes. "*Prostilo*. I'll be there."

"Yes!" I whooped and pumped my fist. She looked at me unimpressed.

"You dropped something," she said, pointing at the floor.

I looked down and saw a spatter of blood that had dripped out of my nose.

Was my nose ever gonna heal?

I learned that 'mensuration' and 'menstruation' were two completely different things thanks to a clarification from Mr. Washy. Everyone stared at me but hey, there are no stupid questions, right? Having been unable to wrap my head around anything else being taught for the rest of the hour I was more than relieved when the bell rang, and with my bag slung over my shoulder I began my march to the rooftop. Along the way came across two familiar faces laughing over a joke I hadn't heard.

"Hey you two, how're you doing?" I asked with a grin that wasn't returned.

The boy turned back to the noticeboard he'd been pinning stuff onto and the girl looked down at the floor, kicking at the back of her heel. "Okay. You?" His tone sounded less like a question and more of a statement.

"I'm doing alright, you seem to be healing well."

He looked at me with no expression I could read.

"What're you working on?" I stepped next to him to admire his handiwork; a collage of brochures and notices, old club posters and portraits of the council members. I notice his and her faces amongst the crowd, Nina's too.

"Nicely done." I nodded.

"I haven't started yet."

Oh.

"Well, good luck then." I nodded, hurrying away. Eager to make my escape.

"Hey." The boy called out and I turned back. He looked at me for a few seconds. "Thanks for helping out with the posters."

"It's no problem. I'm happy to help," I said with a smile.

Stepping onto the rooftop I was more than happy to see Nina sitting amongst her plants. I strolled over, listening to the cheers of the team below and looking at the soft blue sky above. I took a deep breath and sat next to her on the bench. She looked up at me with her tired eyes and gave a weak smile.

"Where's Tobey and Apronas?"

She shrugged. "Apronas told me she had a meeting in town or something. I haven't seen Tobey though."

"He must still be with the pottery teacher." I reasoned, looking out over the school.

"He's taking up poetry now?"

"I guess. You can add that to the roster of whatever else he's doing."

"Like fencing, and skiing..." she started.

"And fishing and wrestling..."

"Painting and archery..."

"Photography and rock climbing..."

"Sewing and farming..."

We both leaned back and sighed. As the list had grown larger and larger so had our smiles as we'd reminisced about all of Tobey's eccentric interests.

"I'm kind of envious," I said.

"Why's that?"

"Doesn't it seem like his life is much more exciting?"

"I suppose, but I'm happy with mine the way it is. Aren't you happy?"

"That's not what I mean," I said, shaking my head.

"What do you mean?"

"Well, can you imagine all those people he knows? Each and everyone one of them could probably never forget that weirdo. Heck, he's probably got way more friends than both of us combined. He wouldn't have a boring day in his life, I bet. He could call up whoever, whenever, and have a day of fun."

"So you'd like more friends? That's easy."

"That's not it either," I sighed, struggling to find the right words. "I guess, I want to mean something. I know I'm not invaluable, but I'm nice to have around."

Nina faced me then, and stared at me with her forest floor eyes.

"Is that what you think?"

"I mean, yeah. I suppose. I don't exactly provide much, do I?"

"What do you mean by that?"

Her eyes were getting harder to meet, so I looked away, favouring the view of the clouds instead. "I don't know. I guess I feel like if I just go, like, if I disappear or something, you guys will be fine. It's kind of comforting in a way, actually."

Nina leaned back and looked at the sky too.

"Sometimes I feel the same way."

I nodded, but then she grabbed my collar and pulled me close, snarling. "But if you *ever* think like that again, if you even *dare* believe that, I'll beat you."

"Uh, y-yes ma'am," I stuttered, but she tightened her grip.

"I'm serious."

"I know."

She sighed, and stared into my eyes. Forest floor.

"I only just got you back."

What did she mean by that?

She lightly shook me.

"Don't go being all sad and moody again, it doesn't suit you."

"Yes ma'am." I nodded.

She released me and went back to resting her head on her hand.

I wasn't sure what to say.

"Want to eat?"

Picture a man with a baseball bat.

She shrugged. "Sure."

He lowered the bat.

With her steady response holding me afloat, I reached into my bookbag and retrieved the lunch I had made. "*That's* what you're gonna feed me?" Nina scoffed, then giggled, poking at the food that had apparently exploded in my lunch box.

"No, it wasn't like this I swear! It must have fallen apart when I fell over."

"Right." She rolled her eyes, but took the chopsticks and lunchbox from my hand and began picking at it.

"What are you doing?"

"I don't want to let the first thing you've ever made me go to waste," she said, popping some rice into her mouth and chewing. "It's really not that bad. Your rice is soft and fluffy, did you use a rice cooker?"

"A rice cooker? Is that what you call the pot?"

"Sorry, I forgot you only use ancient technology," she giggled, playfully smiling. She kept eating and honestly it made me happier than ever that she was enjoying it. She made a fuss, but I'm sure she didn't mind at all that it had been destroyed. I ended up eating the sandwich she'd made for me and we sat together eating amongst her plants.

"David invited us to go watch a movie with him after school tomorrow, wanna come?"

"I can't sorry. I've got practice."

"Come on, please? Skip practice just this once."

"Coach wants me there to practice for the Athletics Appreciation Day next week."

"C'mon Nina, you're already the fastest runner in the school, and the fittest... and the prettiest." I fluttered my eyelids and she shoved my shoulder with a grin she couldn't fight off.

"Fine, I'll come. Just this once."

"Woohoo!" I cheered, throwing my arms into the air.

"Calm down! You're scaring the plants!" she giggled.

Having settled down and sitting beside her once again I remembered something I'd found this morning whilst cleaning. "Check this out." I reached into my bag and retrieved a portable tape player. It was old, that's for sure. I'd never even heard of the musician whose cassette was still jammed in it.

"Woah, where'd you find that?"

"I think it was my Dad's," I answered, handing it to her. She turned it over and touched the buttons one by one. Rubbing her thumb over the rounded edge. "Wanna see if it still works?" I asked, pulling out a set of earphones.

"Sure," she said, and plugged it in. I flipped the switch and a little red light came on, then a whirr sounded as the cassette's reel began spinning. She placed one of the buds in her ear. "I can hear something."

I rotated the volume dial and then I could hear it too, rain and drums. Looped vocals singing with no words. Smooth and clear guitar. The whole arrangement had a crackle that embodied a better time.

"This is good." Nina nodded her head. "Your Dad has good taste."

"Now I think this might've been my Mum's," I joked.

Side by side we sat on the bench, listening to one half of a song each.

"Hey Nina. When you get your license let's go for a drive up the coast. Just me and you."

"I won't be allowed a passenger until next year."

"Then let's break the rules a little bit."

"Maybe." She looked at me.

"What? Is something on my face?"

"No." She shook her head, then cocked it to the side. "I'm just looking at you."

She looked at me like I was the scene from beyond a window. Like I was a butterfly on a petal. Like I was the only thing she wanted to see. The way she looked at me made me feel like I could run again. She made me feel like I was running across a field, through a meadow, through a desert, over the moon. She made me feel like the wind was at my back and my legs worked again.

Nina rested her head on my shoulder.

Chapter Nine
"Overdue apologies."

"Wake up," Nina said, shaking me.

"Huh, what?" I groaned, the cobwebs of my unconscious mind slowly cleared away with each hazy blink. "Where am I?" I shook my head and looked around to find myself on the school rooftop, drenched in a deep orange.

"We fell asleep!" Nina laughed and grabbed my wrist, turning it over to check my watch. "School's been over for two hours!"

"Crap, really?" I rubbed my face and looked at Nina's wild hair. Her bed hair. I'd never seen it this bad before.

It looked good.

"My parents are gonna kill me..." She hung her head. "I've never ditched class before."

"Don't worry about it," I said, yawning. My back was awfully stiff. "They only report you after the third time you've been absent."

"Of course you'd know that," she giggled.

"It's well within my realm of expertise," I replied with a devilish grin.

"There's that smile again," she sighed, and looked at me, forest floor.

"What smile?"

"That evil smile of yours."

Nina said goodbye to her plants and we made our way down to the locker room stretching our cramped limbs along the way. Fresh from practice was David standing at his locker.

"Yo, my man. What's up?' I said, but he didn't turn around. "David?"

"Huh? Oh hey, what's up?" He nodded at me, distracted. He had the pink envelope in his hand and had just been reading the letter.

"What's that?" Nina asked.

"I think it's a confession letter. But it doesn't say who it's from."

'Funny, I–" I stopped myself as all the pieces fell into place. "Ohhhh."

"What?"

"Nothing." I shook my head. "What's it say?"

"Whoever wrote it says that she'll confess to me at the festival this Saturday."

"What festival?" I asked, and they both turned to me.

"What do you mean, 'what festival'?" David scoffed.

"How could you forget? It's all anybody ever talks about," Nina said, shaking her head.

"All you freaks talk about are teleporters and sewer dolphins!" I cried out in response.

"He does have a point." David nodded. Nina held her hand out and he shook it.

"No, dummy. The letter."

His face went scarlet, but he handed it over and she skimmed through.

"Huh."

"What?"

"I didn't know your middle name was Vernon."

"Where does it say that?" I asked, and she pointed to the first four words on the letter.

Dear David Vernon Evergreen.

"Hardly anybody knows what my middle name is." He shrugged.

"It must mean that someone close to you wrote this," Nina speculated, handing it back. "So what are you going to do?"

"I'm not sure. I kind of already have my eye on someone."

Oh crap.

"Go, man!"

I said that a bit hastily.

"It'd be rude not to," I lamely added.

"So who do you like then?" Nina asked, biting her lip and raising an eyebrow.

"Wouldn't you like to know, " he smirked.

I whispered in Nina's ear and she gasped.

"No way, really! You're not lying?" she asked me as she jumped in place, hands rapidly clapping.

"Nope. That's one hundred percent truth."

"What is?" David asked, looking between the two of us. "What did you just say?"

"You *have* to go!" Nina giggled, patting his arms. "Do it for me as an early birthday present!"

"I don't even know when your birthday is, " he said dismissively, then turned to me and grabbed my shirt, shaking me but pleading desperately. "Please, you have to tell me man. What do you know, what do you knooooooooow?"

"Are you sure you know what you're doing?" Nina asked, standing in the doorway of the kitchen. I had reassured her many times that I was confident in my abilities but it did nothing to dissuade her reservations, though I couldn't exactly blame her with *my* track record. I mean, it was nothing compared to Tobey's, but it was bad enough to garner concern.

"I'm following the recipe step-by-step, so if it turns out bad don't blame me, blame the book," I said and she sighed.

"I'm surprised you can even read," she muttered as I attempted to chop an onion. "Why did you decide to follow a Europan recipe anyway?"

I shrugged. "It's good eatin'."

"Don't cut it like that," she warned and stepped forward, wrapping her hands around mine. "You hold the onion like this so it doesn't slip as you cut into it."

I did as she instructed and found it a lot easier to cut through, but it didn't help at all when it came to the stinging at my eyes and the resulting tears.

"You're helpless," she laughed before helping rinse out my eyes. "You're supposed to have a bowl of water next to you when cutting onions, didn't your mother teach you that?"

No. She didn't teach me much about anything.

"Why are there so many rules for cooking?" I complained with a sniffle. "We should just go back to eating raw meat off of animal carcasses."

"I'm not sure what you've been watching but we've never done that." She giggled. "Besides, I know you'd miss my cooking too much."

"That's true."

With my eyes cleaned out, the meat, sauces and co. were left to simmer, and the pasta was on the boil with the egg timer sitting next to it, ticking away. I stretched and grinned, pleased with how well it was going. Other than the assault on my eyes courtesy of the onion, everything else had been smooth sailing. It wasn't long after that we were sitting around the coffee table slurping down noodles and watching some rather poorly funded game show on TV. As the show cut away to an advertisement about some rather long candy, Nina looked at me.

"How's your nose?"

"It's a lot better than it was."

"Let me have a look at it," she said, and crawled around the table. Reaching out, she gently touched my face. "Does it still hurt?"

"When you poke it, yeah."

"Sorry." She retracted her hand.

Suddenly, I remembered something.

"Oh, I forgot to tell you."

"What?"

"You were right."

"About what?"

"I saw another Time-Pauser."

"You what!?" she shrieked, and leapt onto my lap, wrapping her arms around me and squeezing me tight. "I was right! I was right!" she cheered, bobbing from side to side. Then she grabbed my collar and shook me.

What was with everyone doing that recently?

"Tell me about it! Who are they?"

"I uh, I don't know," I said meekly.

"How do you not know?" she yelled, "when did you see them?"

"Last week... Wednesday I think." She shook me again.

"You're only telling me now!?"

"I forgot!"

"Ugh!" She groaned. "Tell me everything!"

"Alright, sheesh." I rolled my eyes. "Before I met you guys in that cafe I was talking to Lucy and there was a Pause, and while I was waiting there someone ran past so I followed them. It turns out there are two others like me. I didn't see either of their faces, but I managed to talk to the girl."

"What did she say?" Her face lit up, and filled with excitement she jumped up and down. "What did she say!?"

"Calm down! I'm getting to it..." I muttered, trying to ignore the fact she was still on my lap. "She was crazy fast, I struggled to keep up with her, but after I almost fell off a roof–"

"-Is that why your ribs hurt?" she said, poking my chest.

"Yes," I hissed, "anyways, she pulled me up and we spoke a little bit. She was rude and evasive, and didn't answer any of my questions, but she did confirm that there were three of us in total."

"That's incredible!" Nina grinned. Her face was awfully close to mine. "Three Time-Pausers! I can't believe it! Did she know why you guys can pause time?"

"No. She didn't know that."

"That's a pity. Have you seen them since?"

"Nope. Not even once."

She ran her fingers through her hair and shook her head in disbelief. "That's incredible... I can't believe it... It's not just you! There's three! Three!"

"Uh huh." I nodded. "I'm aware."

"What can you tell me about her? What does she look like?"

"I already told you that I didn't see her face, but she was young. She could even go to the same school as us. "

"I wonder who it is... I'll have to investigate!" she said with a beaming grin. "I'm so happy I could kiss you!" She gripped my collar and stared at me, breathing heavily.

I stared at her, unsure what to say.

Pressure was mounting as the seconds of silence grew longer and longer.

"Your uh, your nose is bleeding." She recoiled, laughing as she crawled off of me. "I'll get you a tissue."

Phew, crisis averted. Relief washed over me and I felt my soul return to my body. My blood pressure had been spiking and I'm not sure how much longer I was going to remain conscious.

"I still can't believe it," Nina mumbled as she returned to the room. "That explains all the teleporter rumours, right? If there's a boy and a girl it makes perfect sense!"

"Yeah, yeah." I said, taking the tissue from her outstretched hand and plugging my nose.

That explains a lot, actually.

"It's all true..."

"I'm aware." I said. "So, do you wanna finish that game?"

"What game?"

I pointed at the TV.

"Oh right. Yeah, sure," she said, shaking her head. I pulled out the console and we began to play, but the entire time she kept muttering to herself, coming up with new theories that I didn't care for. While I fought against shadow monsters and moved boxes Nina asked me a steady stream of questions, the answers of which were jotted down in her red notebook. Even after another two hours spent exploring the bastille I felt no closer to the end. I saved, and seeing the two in-game characters sleeping on the couch Nina and I both yawned. She reached for my hand and read the time off my watch.

"Oh, jinkies. It's way later than I thought."

I turned the console off and lay on the floor, only now feeling the fatigue plaguing my body. "Nina?"

"Yes?"

"I don't think I ever apologized," I said, but she didn't reply. Instead she just cocked her head and watched me. "I'm sorry for pushing you over."

"What are you talking about?" Her voice was curious, and sweet.

I rolled onto my side and looked into her eyes.

"Are you really talking about *back then*?" she asked, and looked at me with concern. "What made you think about that?"

I couldn't blame her for being surprised. '*Back then*' wasn't a topic I liked delving into, but recently I'd been thinking about it more and more. That was around the same time I'd properly met her too, and it didn't exactly introduce myself in the nicest way. I wasn't the nicest person back then. "Yes, I am. I'm sorry."

She gave me a sad smile, and placed her hand on my face. It was warm, and so damn soft it felt like a dream. "You don't need to apologize. I forgave you long ago. I hope you haven't been feeling guilty."

I closed my eyes and focused on her hand.

"I forgive you, dummy," she said, and her thumb stroked my cheek. I could hear her moving and I felt her hair fall across my face, tickling my nose. I was scared to open my eyes so I just sat there, doing nothing as I felt her breathing softly. Lips on my forehead, a gentle kiss. With that simple gesture I felt like my sins had been cleansed, and I shattered in her arms. A single tear escaped my eye and she stroked it away with her thumb. "Don't feel guilty. I'm happy that I know you."

I opened my eyes and found forest floor mere inches from mine. Her tired eyes and soft smile helped keep my heart together, and she was so close I could have counted the freckles that dotted her nose.

"*It's getting pretty late,*" she whispered. "*Is it okay if I stay the night?*"

"Uh, sure. You can sleep in my sister's room if you want."

"That's perfect."

Chapter Ten

"Something a little too familiar."

Nina had already gone when I'd woken up, having left a letter informing me that she'd left early for school and that breakfast was in the kitchen. I felt like I was missing something, but shook the thought from my mind and munched down on the toast she'd left me on the way to school. I was early this day too, and as such the sky was still a rich baby blue. It was home to clouds that looked too lazy to form any shapes, and I knew exactly how they felt. Whilst walking alongside my classmates but having no one to converse with my gaze turned to the calm sea. The wind brought the familiar smell of salt to my nose, which was feeling a lot better today.

"Morning." Tobey welcomed me, looking at his watch again. "That makes it two days in a row you've managed to be on time."

"The first two of many to come," I said with a grin. "So how are you? Do anything interesting last night?"

"Well, I knitted a picture of a tiger using ancient techniques taught to me by a travelling scribe," he mentioned nonchalantly, "then I had caviar with the mayor. He's quite a nice fellow actually."

I gave him a sideways glance, but couldn't tell if he was joking.

"What about you?" he asked, "how was your night?"

"It was nice. Nina and I had some dinner, talked, played videogames. The usual."

"Did she stay the night?"

"How did you know that?"

"I just know things, O-boy," he said with an enigmatic grin and a tap of his nose. "I know many, many things."

"Why do you know many, many things?"

"It's my job." He shrugged his shoulders. "Simple as that."

I shook my head. The heat was starting to get to me, and I fluffed my collar.

"We should get a watermelon."

Tobey looked at me and nodded. "I agree."

I closed my eyes and began to imagine it, green skin with dark stripes. "A big one."

"We should crack it open with a big stick."

"We could invite everyone over too. Have a melon eating party."

"There's such a thing?"

I winked at Tobey. "Didn't you know?"

David was talking to Eileen beneath the shedding oak trees, and as we walked past I heard snippets of their conversation. He was showing her the pink envelope and asking her what she thought he should do, and all the while her face was red and she was looking away. I shook my head and sighed with a smile. Just admit it and get it over with, I thought.

"It's pretty obvious." Tobey said.

"That it is," I agreed, and made my way to my locker. During the process of putting my shoes on David came by and slapped my shoulder.

"Still on for the movies tonight?" He asked, and reminded by the plans made yesterday I practically cheered. "I'll take that as a yes," he laughed and strode away.

"Movies, movies, movies, we're going to the movies~" I sung to myself. I was then approached by another person, this time female, and blonde.

"Hey." Lucy smiled. "Are you free tomorrow?"

"Sure am, why?"

"Wanna come to a karaoke bar?"

"Shouldn't you be, I don't know, studying?"

"We'll be studying..." she mumbled, then she gave me a meek glance. "Inbetween songs."

"That doesn't sound terribly efficient," I laughed, placing my shoes in the locker and shutting the door.

"That doesn't matter." She pouted. "So are you coming?"

"I think I'll pass. Singing and I don't get along so well."

"Now I *have* to hear you sing! Please come, please?"

I stared at her.

"Please please pleeeeease?" She begged, bowing her head in a dramatic fashion.

How could I resist such a tempting offer?

"Fine, I'll come," I said resignedly and she jumped in the air, cheering.

"Awesome! I'll text you the details okay? Don't chicken out!" She ran off, her blonde hair bouncing energetically.

"Lady man, aren't you?" Apronas said as she strolled past. Her tone judgemental.

"Oh please, you're the one always clinging to me!" I yelled and she scoffed.

Shaking my head I made my way into class.

When the bell rang I whooped so loud in excitement that Mr. Washy almost jumped out of his socks. He clutched at his heart with rather stubby arms as I shouted: "One hour closer to the movies!" I slung my bag over my shoulder and walked over to Tobey. "Coming?"

"Yeah, in a moment. Go ahead." He said.

He was sitting at his desk with nothing on the top. No book, no encyclopaedia, no phone. I wasn't sure exactly what he was doing but he appeared to be waiting for something. I chalked it up to being a new Tobey eccentricity and patted him on the shoulder. "Sure thing. See you later bud."

Strolling out of class I was in such a good mood that I wanted to whistle a tune, but which one? As I browsed the library of songs I'd memorized, searching for one that best fit the tone of mood I was currently in, I began the march to the rooftop. I wanted to see Nina's face, and her smile. I wanted to see Nina again.

I heard a yell, then something crash somewhere in the stairwell below me.

Leaning over the barrier I could see Oscar throw someone against a wall whilst his snarling laugh echoed up the stairwell, chilling my blood. Immediately I rushed down. I considered leaping over the barrier and attempting to look cool, but I didn't want to slip and embarrass myself. I came to a stop and Oscar turned around, and as his eyes settled on me he sneered.

"You..." I glanced behind him and saw the poster boy slumped against a wall, nose bleeding, eyes closed. "You disgust me the most..." Oscar continued.

He tapped something against his thigh and I looked down to see the shiny blade of a knife in his hand. Everything in my body froze, and the hair on the back of my neck stood on end. This was too much. I wanted to run but I felt locked in place, like I was in a nightmare.

"After everything I did to you, you never retaliated. *He* at least brought a knife," Oscar said, bringing my attention back to him. He stared at me with ice-blue eyes and tossed the knife onto the ground. It clanged and slid across the floor, coming to a stop as it bumped into my shoe.

"Pick it up," he commanded, but I shook my head. "I want you to pick it up. I want you to stab me. I want you to kill me. I know you want to." I stared at the knife, but I kept shaking my head. "Do what you didn't do *then*." He reached into his coat and pulled out a knife of his own. "Do it, fight me!" He screamed as he rushed forward, colliding with me and shoving me against a wall. The wind was knocked out of my lungs and a familiar pain came back. He pinned one arm against my throat, choking me, but I kept the one with the knife at bay, gripping his wrist with all my strength.

"I know you can fight, I've seen it before," he said through gritted teeth. "Stop being so pathetic!" He applied more force against my neck and I choked. The knife edged closer. *"Don't you remember?"* he whispered, spittle landing on my cheek. *"Don't you remember that summer with... Ophelia?"*

I glared into his eyes and he knew he'd struck a nerve. One still exposed after two years. I looked behind him but the boy was still slumped over, unmoving. He would be of no help. Oscar pulled me back and slammed my head against the wall.

"Look at me!" he roared, and my eyes met his. "Why didn't you fight? Didn't you love her enough!?" My brain was getting cloudy; I was running out of air. "I gave you a once in a lifetime opportunity and you squandered it, you lost the girl of your dreams. I had her! Her lips brushed mine, remember? She pulled me to her and—"

I launched my head forward and our skulls collided in an explosion of pain and for a second I was blind. Both of his hands reached to his forehead as he stumbled backwards and I heard the knife clatter against the floor. "That's it! That's what I've been waiting for!" he laughed.

I ran towards the stairs and he dived towards the knife.

I pushed myself. Run faster, faster! I was always faster than Oscar, keep going! All the way to the landing I could hear his footsteps echoing louder and louder behind me but I didn't stop to see how close he was before I jumped. He probably wasn't expecting me to leap, but I definitely wasn't expecting him to come along.

When I landed halfway down the flight he crashed into me and my leg buckled. Together we spun and rolled down the stairs. The corners dug into my bones and pain ricocheted across my body as my head crunched against the stairwell and Oscar's limbs bumped against my own. As we hit the ground below we came apart, and the rolling came to a stop.

I groaned softly, as my face lay against the cool, hardwood floor. There wasn't an inch of my body that didn't ache, and I could tell that tomorrow morning wasn't going to be kind. Am I dead? Am I finally dead? I thought to myself. No. Being dead couldn't hurt *this* much.

I didn't move, I didn't get up, I didn't do anything, I didn't have any energy left, so I just listened as Oscar got to his feet. "That hurt. I guess we aren't kids anymore, huh?" he muttered, and I didn't even bother to respond. I heard his steps get closer until he stopped above me. I was struggling to breathe, shallow breaths were all I could muster, and being unable to move meant there was nothing I could do if he were to grab my neck and choke me to death. There was nothing I could do.

He grunted, as if he'd just noticed something. "Where's your phone?" he asked. When I didn't respond he sighed and squatted down, then rifled through my pockets. I felt myself growing warmer, and yet colder as I lay there.

From my phone came three beeps.

"Yes, hello? I'd like to request an ambulance. My friend has been stabbed."

Friend, I scoffed.

Wait, what? Stabbed?

"Yes, there is quite a lot of blood."

I tried to move but he stood on my back and pushed me back down.

"*Don't move, you'll only make it worse,*" he whispered, and it was then that I saw the red pool peeking out from beneath my arms. It slowly encroached closer and closer, staining my nice white, ironed shirt. I couldn't help but feel as if all that blood should be inside me instead, but there was nothing much I could do. There was nothing I could do but listen as Oscar told them our location. Exhaustion set in like a heavy blanket even as I lay there doing nothing.

The world had gone silent and I couldn't hear anything except for my own weakened heartbeat. Oscar wasn't talking and I couldn't hear cheering or singing. For a moment I thought that I had lost my hearing, but I slowly came to the realization that time was paused. My dulled senses weren't alert enough to inform me of the change. I watched as the pool of blood grew larger and larger, and even as my vision was getting blurry I noticed a figure appear at the top of the steps. It watched me for a few seconds before walking away, and time resumed promptly.

"What's that girl's number? What's her name again... Nina?" Oscar asked, then shook his head. "Don't worry, I'll find it."

Tobey came into view and he grabbed my hand, placing his fingers against my wrist. Maybe he was testing the strength of my pulse. "You'll be fine O-boy, just relax, okay?" he said softly. He was tousling my hair and telling me it was all going to be okay for what felt like forever until Nina shoved him out of the way and dropped to her knees.

"No, no no... Tell me you're okay!" she screamed and rolled me over.

Be careful... You're getting my blood all over you...

She held my head against her chest and cradled me, rocking me gently in her arms all the while screaming at Oscar. I found it hard to listen. Not only because my senses were getting duller by the second as my grasp on consciousness waned, but also because I'd never heard her cry like this before. It was making my little black heart shatter as I heard her desperately whisper my name again and again and again. Her tears fell onto my face and she wiped them away with her thumb, and she struggled to hold my dead weight. I'm dying, aren't I? My limbs were all for show, and though I wanted to hold her hand I couldn't even move. I tried to speak but the words wouldn't come. I wanted to say something, to thank Tobey, to curse Oscar, to tell her I loved her. Anything.

But nothing came. Nothing at all.

Lying there I saw her forest floor eyes and I felt like it was okay.

But I didn't want to let go.

Chapter Eleven

"Alive again."

The faint, rhythmic beeping of the machine monitoring my heart was the first thing I became aware of. A little while later I noticed the soft, uneven breathing of someone sleeping. It took a long time for me to gather the energy to open my eyes, and it didn't help that my head ached just as bad as my body. When my eyelids finally parted they revealed a hospital room. One of those small, private ones. The blinds were closed, but a sliver of brilliant light shone through, illuminating golden specks of dust and settling across Nina's shoulders. She was leaning on my bed, her head on her hands and fast asleep. Heaving with such an effort it felt like I was climbing out of my own grave, I lifted my hand and stretched my fingers then rested it on top of Nina's head. I played with her hair, rolling a lock of hair over my thumb. It didn't take long for me to notice how stiff my muscles were, and the IV needle stuck in my arm.

Nina's hair was always a mess, but her usual bed hair had been taken to the eleventh degree and I couldn't help but smile. It suited her. I didn't move for a few minutes, enjoying the stillness and the softness of her hair.

Just how close had I come to death? Close enough to be handed a personal invitation actually. And how long had I been here?

Someone I hadn't noticed stood up, and with a wave and a smile I realized it was Tobey. I tried to speak but only a breathless croak escaped my mouth and he put a finger to his lips. He walked over slowly and quietly, and leaned in to whisper in my ear.

"I told you that you'd be fine, didn't I? It's good to see you awake again," he said with a smile. *"Nina's gonna wake up soon so I'll give you two some privacy."* He patted my shoulder then made his way out of the room and I returned my gaze to Nina. As I stroked her hair she stirred,

and I watched her eyelids flutter as she came to. For a moment she looked confused, then when she remembered where she was her head snapped up and her eyes locked onto mine. Forest floor. She gasped and launched herself at me, and I weakly chuckled, trying not to complain about how tightly she was squeezing me.

"I was so worried..." she said, her voice muffled by my shoulder. I ran my fingers through her hair and held her as she trembled, then all of a sudden she grabbed me by the collar and pulled me up. "You're not allowed to do that again!" she yelled, staring intensely at me, lip quivering. Her eyes that always looked like they were on the verge of crying were.

"Don't worry, I'd rather not," I laughed weakly.

When Tobey came back he had a nurse in tow, who he was on a first-name basis with, and she briefly checked on my vitals as they chatted before vacating my room. Nina and Tobey then spent the next few hours explaining how Oscar had been heralded as a hero for alerting the authorities and that David, Eileen, Lucy and Apronas had all been here to visit me. I thought that explained the basket of flowers sitting atop a spare set of David's gym clothes. Nina also obtained a tray of hospital food and I felt like a king as she placed grape after grape in my mouth.

"Oh, you'll be happy about this," Nina said with a smile. "Enricho decided to run after Isabella, and Miss. Colione decided to let them leave after seeing how happy they were together."

"You watched TV while I was dying?"

"We watched it together, dummy." She pointed at the TV sitting in the corner of the room.

"They tried to get her to leave once visiting hours were over but she refused to budge," Tobey said, grinning. "She fought them all off and told them that she would die before she left your side."

“Oh shut up,” Nina said with a blush blossoming across her cheeks. “He’s being dramatic.”

“Thanks,” I chuckled.

“So... did you see anything?” Tobey asked. “Like an angel or anything?”

Nina punched his arm and gasped. “Tobey!”

“What, I was just curious...” he muttered.

“I can’t remember much," I said, scratching my nose. "But I think I remember a television, or something."

Tobey nodded.

"You watch too much TV!" Nina giggled.

The door opened and a doctor came in. She had long beautiful blonde hair and a familiar face, and her voice was gentle on the ears. It was Lucy’s mother!

“Good evening. It’s reassuring to see that you’re conscious and responsive,” she said, checking the clipboard hung on the foot of the bed. “It’s good to see you again, although I would prefer if it were under better circumstances.” She gave a weak laugh. “You were lucky your friend called, I’m not sure how much longer you could have been left there.”

“Some *friend*,” Nina scoffed, and Lucy’s Mother looked at her oddly.

“It says here that you suffered a concussion, multiple bone bruises, and that your abdomen was punctured.”

That’s a fancy way of saying I’d been stabbed.

She flipped the paper over. “It also says here that your nose had been broken recently, and that you had a few cracked ribs. Is there any particular reason you didn’t check in to be seen for those?” she asked.

“Because he’s an idiot.” Tobey and Nina said in unison.

Lucy’s Mother smiled politely. “Okay... It seems that they’re healing well, extraordinarily well in fact. Curious... I suppose you must be very healthy.” She remarked before checking all the little dials and readings on the fancy machines I'd been hooked up to, and scribbling down whatever relevant information she'd seen onto the checklist.

"You must have some friends in high places, this room was very expensive to pay for," she said nonchalantly.

"Wait, what? Someone paid for this room?" Nina asked.

Tobey also turned to face her. "Who?"

"I can't remember the name..." she mumbled, "it was something really exotic though. I wouldn't even try pronouncing it."

Appronas?

It appeared Tobey had the same idea as he and I shared a confused expression. When Lucy's Mother finished with my checkup she wished me a speedy recovery as she made her exit.

"Did she say Apronas paid for the room?" Nina pondered.

"She's the only foreigner we know," I said, "I guess I owe her a thanks."

"How could she afford it though?"

"Maybe she's part of a drug empire and she's come over here to expand her influence on behalf of the family," Tobey said with a stone-faced expression, and we shook our heads at him.

"Don't be stupi... wait, can you guys hear that?" I said, faintly aware of a buzzing sound. Nina began looking around the room for whatever the source of the noise was, but Tobey beelined it straight for the little plastic bag full of my belongings sitting on the chair in the corner. He flipped my phone open and looked at the screen.

"It says 'Mum and Dad.'"

"Well don't just stand there, give it to him!" Nina shouted and he immediately rushed to my side, giving me the phone. I answered the call and put it up to my ear.

"Hello?" I croaked.

"Oh good." I heard my mum sigh. "Are you okay? What happened?"

"Just lost some blood is all. Nothing too serious," I replied.

"That's a relief," she said, sighing again.

My dad chuckled but I could tell it wasn't genuine. "Just a few gallons, eh boy? Nothing to strong men like us."

"Something like that."

"Is Nina there?" my mum asked. My eyes flicked over to her.

"Yes."

"Goodness, that's so cute! Tell her I said hi!"

I rolled my eyes. I'm glad they were enjoying themselves.

"Listen son," my dad said, "we were driving along the Moeno when we got the call, and we've decided to end our trip short and head home next week to check up on you."

"You don't have to, really."

They really didn't.

"Nonsense, what kind of parents would we be if we didn't come?"

"I love you darling, heal well and stay out of trouble, okay?"

"Wait, no, you don't have to–"

They hung up on me and I sighed. That was just so typical of them. Doing whatever they wanted whenever they wanted. Apparently severe medical injuries were the only thing that would make my parents bother to stop by for a visit.

I looked at Nina.

"Mum says hi."

I had convinced Nina and Tobey to go home, have a shower, and sleep in a real bed, but I have to admit I was still surprised when I found out the person who opened the door in the middle of the night waking me up wasn't either of them. Two people entered my room shrouded in silhouette, and judging from the lack of beeping emanating from the heart monitor, time was paused. They were the other Pausers.

They came to a stop at the foot of the bed, standing side-by side.

"Are you awake?"

"Somewhat."

"Thank you, for what you did," said the girl.

"For both of us," added the boy. "If only more people were as kind as you, then the sharp corners wouldn't hurt as much."

As I lay there, I thought that his voice was familiar.

The girl stepped forward, approaching as soft as a whisper. I turned to watch her as she got closer. "It's fortunate that you are one of us. If you find that your heart lies with ours, then you can join us in the space we find for ourselves." She stopped right next to me and leaned in, her shadowy form growing as she came closer. She spoke so softly that I strained to listen, and she was so close her warm breath tickled my neck. She smelt like strawberries.

"*No matter what the future holds, or what choices we make, even if TV's learn to walk or the world forgets our existence, let's promise to become more than the labels people put on our backs.*"

Then came a kiss that landed on my cheek. Her lips were soft and warm and I felt myself blush, even under the circumstances. She giggled quietly, and brought a hand up to tousle my hair. I wanted to say something, but I wasn't sure *what*, exactly. She retreated back to the other end of the room and we stayed like that for a minute. Other than the time she had saved me, this was the closest I had gotten to another person who could pause time.

"Who are you?" I finally asked.

"You'll find out soon enough," they answered.

"Then... what do you want?"

"You'll find out soon enough."

Chapter Twelve
"Foodcourt Chic."

I was standing on the roof watching the city below when a woman with a white shirt, a black tie, and hair half-up-half-down that was always unkempt came to me. Her hair wasn't 'Nina bed hair' unkempt, it was 'stressed and overwhelmed' unkempt. She had a pointed face and a thin body, and she carried herself with an energetic attitude I'm sure she was forcing. There was no way she *wasn't* forcing it.

"Heyyyyyy, how're you holding up kiddo? Long time no see, huh? Although, I guess that's for the best," she lamely chuckled with forced cheer, attempting and failing to hide how nervous she was. She spoke a lot more fluently, but her accent was still terrible even after all these years. After assaulting my eardrums with it the first time two years ago, I asked where she was from and she'd explained that she'd come from some place called the Lake Cities. Why or how she'd come here, I have no idea.

"You been keeping well, Laine?" I asked.

"It's *Senior Detective Laine* now," she said with a pained chuckle, "but yes. I'm well. I've been very busy."

"I see," I said, rather disinterested. I knew why she was here, and she knew that I wouldn't be in particularly high spirits talking about it, and she definitely knew that I wouldn't be in any mood to suffer through her small talk.

"They put me on your case again."

She attempted to make it sound like a good thing.

"Hooray," I muttered and she sighed, hanging her head. She was always moving with such exaggerated motions that annoyed me. Maybe that's just how they were in the Lake Cities, or maybe it was just her. Either way it got on my nerves.

Senior Detective Laine leaned on the railing beside me and rested her head on her hands, looking out at the city and the blue sky above. "Look kiddo... I know it's a sore subject but I have to ask, okay?"

"Okay."

There was a kid far below holding onto a kite as it swung wildly, surfing the wind. It was bright red and shaped like a diamond. I had one like that once.

"So this Oscar kid's involved again, huh? He said he found you like that, with the knife in your back. He also said he tried to remove it which is why his fingerprints were on the handle, but I think I know better. He was the one who did it, right?"

"What else did you hear?"

"That your friends Nina and Tobey were second on the scene. Both of their accounts of the situation concur that Oscar was there first, although neither saw him stab you. They also mentioned he wasn't acting violently. And that he was on the phone to the emergency services when they arrived."

"He was," I confirmed, and she nodded, wanting more information.

"So... did he do it? Was he the one who stabbed you? I know you and this kid got history–"

"-Was it his knife in me?" I interrupted.

"Er, uh no. Well, that's the thing. It gets a little muddy on the details here..." She glanced at me. "Are you listening?"

I sighed. "Yes."

"There's two big pieces of evidence we found. But they're not just big, they're immense, massive. They could potentially solve a massive crime spree. "

"Just spit it out already."

I was being a bit cruel, wasn't I?

"Okay." She nodded her head and fiddled with her badge, which is something I'd noticed she did to comfort herself. "We found some blood that didn't belong to either you or Oscar on the floor above, and the knife that was used to attack you fits the data profile of the knife that's been used in multiple attacks in the recent weeks."

I spun to face her. "What?"

"I said–"

"-No, what do you mean?"

"The knife that was used in the attack fits the profile of the weapon that's been used in multiple slashings across town. I'm sure you've heard about it on the news."

I shook my head in disbelief.

"Laine."

"Yes?"

"There *was* someone else there, a boy from my school. I don't know his name but he's part of the school committee. His picture's up on the wall. Oscar's the one who stabbed me but it was *his* knife."

"H-holy crap," she stuttered. Shaking her head from side to head. She always did that when faced with a realization. "A-Are y-you sure?"

"Yes I'm sure!" I shouted. "Oscar had beaten the guy unconscious but I'm sure it was him!"

"This is big, thanks kiddo!" she yelled from halfway across the rooftop as she ran back inside.

This is big indeed.

This is not just big, it's immense, it's *massive.*

But I was too tired to handle it.

I didn't even want to have anything to do with it in the first place.

Eh, whatever. It was in someone else's hands now.

Not my problem anymore.

David's clothes were a bit too big for me on account of all his extra muscles. This wasn't the only annoyance I'd had on the long walk home, as upon putting my shoes on I realized that they were still soggy; soaked with my blood. So I ended up walking home with all my bloodstained personal belongings in a plastic bag packed on top of a flower basket, and only one sock on my feet. I reasoned that it was far less suspicious than looking like a walking crime scene. Also a lot more hygienic than giving my feet a literal blood bath. Different parts of my body would ache with each step or each turn.

Life is pain, and I'm The Goddesses' punching bag... But hey, I live for the suffering.

I had only been released in the afternoon, and with my stomach growling like a wild animal I knew I wouldn't make it home without something in the tank, so I stopped for something big and greasy to eat. Odd looks were shot my way, but I ignored them as I chowed down my Lovely Burger. I'd heard that this particular chain was a favourite of Miss. Morina Winslow's.

I guess you could say I have brand loyalty.

I was taking the walk slowly, under orders from the doctor, so the sky was dyed a rich orange only halfway home. Loose stones, usually nothing more than something that bounced off my shoe became a devious enemy, poking at my feet like little spears and latching on with their teeth. Before long I found myself hobbling as they chewed through my last remaining sock.

"Having fun?"

Akera was sitting on a guard rail, facing the sunset and blowing smoke. I expected her to be smiling, finding joy in the pain and awkwardness I was suffering from, but the corners of her mouth weren't even tilted up a little bit.

"That's not exactly the word I'd use for it," I said in reply.

She swung her arm around and a pair of shoes came bouncing across the tarmac towards me. How uncharacteristically generous. This was new. I gingerly knelt down to grab the pair and walked over to her.

"If the police ask, you didn't get them from me," she said, and I stopped for a moment. She was only joking, right? Probably. They weren't exactly my size, but it was a hell of a lot better than walking on the rocks barefoot. I slowly climbed over the guardrail, wincing as my wound stretched, and while she watched me the whole time she didn't throw any insults my way, and when I had finished the world's worst gymnastics performance she held her hand out, offering me her cigarette.

"At least we'll know if I'm still airtight," I said, and she laughed so suddenly I got a fright. The harshness of it almost made me believe that she'd forgotten how to.

"If nothing else, at least you're a little funny," she said with a wide smile on her face as she looked out over the bay. "I don't give you enough credit, honestly."

"Mmhmm," I murmured, breathing in the foul air and wondering why I smoked these little tar sticks. Maybe I just hated myself. I handed it back. "So were you waiting for me or did you just happen to have a pair of extra shoes?"

"Wouldn't you like to know?" came her reply, although this time it sounded like a smile.

"You just wanted to make me work for them, didn't you?"

Another laugh. Hm. Maybe she was developing some gallows humour because on any other day she'd lambast me for saying the same thing. We sat there for a few minutes, passing the cigarette between each other as we watched the sun hover above the sea. The wind gently tugged at our clothes, just to let us know that it was still there.

"So uh, what are you gonna do about Dan?" I asked as I scratched my stitches.

"I don't know," she sighed, "there's no way I can make that much money in two days."

When I asked her how much she owed I couldn't do much to argue.

"Don't worry, he's mostly harmless."

A certain memory of mine said otherwise, but I didn't argue.

"Why do you owe him that much money?"

"'Cause of my brother. He was Dan's gopher, but the idiot got into an accident and he hasn't woken up in months. The bills kept piling up so I had to start working for Dan to keep up. One little slip-up was all it took."

I nodded. "Are you still mad at Lucy?" I asked hesitantly, reaching for the cigarette.

"No, not at all. It was a little silly of me, honestly. I'm glad she's getting back into the groove of things. She was really down for a while there."

"Howcome?"

"I think all the pressure got to her, like what her parents expected of her and all that. They're real nice people, it was all in her head. But something happened between her and a boy. I don't know the details but she's a lot stronger now. I don't think it'll bother her as much."

"Who?"

She shrugged.

I nodded with lungs full of tar. "I'm glad you were there for her."

She looked at me, smiled, then punched me. "Don't get all soft on me now!"

I rubbed my shoulder, pretending it hurt. "Don't worry, I wouldn't dare."

For a moment I thought I'd left my house keys somewhere and patted myself down in a frantic panic, sighing with relief in dramatic fashion when I finally found them in my blood bag. I turned the lock and ah, home sweet home. Nothing had changed but it seemed somehow different; like I hadn't been there in a long time. Furniture with cloth patterns that I had long since memorized now seemed so alien, and none of the rooms seemed to be in the right place. I sat down in the foyer and pressed play on the answering machine as I took off Akera's shoes. They had begun to chafe my poor feet, but I was more than appreciative of the gift.

"Hey O-boy! This is Money, you remember me right? Anyway, I'm calling from Wayward Videos to let you know that your VHS copies of 'Peperiia', 'A tale of Two Flies', and one... 'Schoolgirl's Naughty Adventures' are overdue. You gotta return those, man, lest you get a feeee~ Anyway, drop by whenever. I'll scrub your bill, consider it a favour for a friend. Alright, Money out."

I laid down after freeing my feet and listened to the rest of the messages. When did I get so popular? I thought, though most of them were just businesses. Then I heard a voice say my name. A voice I hadn't heard in years.

"...? I heard what happened, the hospital called me. They couldn't get in contact with mum and dad so I had to let them know. They were, well, *their usual selves*. I hope you're okay... It's Otille by the way, but I'm sure you guessed that. Well I *hoped* you guessed that anyway. If you're listening to this then that's a good sign... It's boring out here in the 'big city'. Well, I shouldn't say that. It's only boring sometimes. I've made some pretty good friends here. We go to a lot of art galleries and stuff, the kind of places you hate. I'm dating a guy called Tsutomu, he's really sweet. He gives me flowers every time we go on a date... Goddesses I miss you, I really hope you're okay. If you're listening to this, call me back okay? I need to hear your voice. I'm sorry I haven't called. I could say I'm too busy but then I'd just be lying. I've been a pretty crappy big sister, I'm sorry. We should try to organize a visit sometime. I love you. Call me back, okay?"

After the machine beeped and fell silent I got to my feet. Deleting all the messages but one before hobbling over to the couch and taking my time sitting down carefully. I was wary of ripping and tearing my stitches. After the TV took a second to warm up the six o'clock news appeared and was stretched over the curves of my CRT screen. They were talking about the slashings that had been happening in town.

Apparently there had been even more. I fought a shiver that stretched down my spine and flicked over to the Home Network Channel where Miss. Morina Winslow was trying to sell what appeared to be a hula hoop with tassels. She was giving a pretty convincing argument.

I sighed as I reached for my phone and thumbed in Otille's number. I listened to the dial tone.

I didn't even realize I had fallen asleep until I heard a loud set of jangling keys followed by my front door being loudly opened. I began to wake as a crowd of voices entered and I was blinded as someone turned on the light.

"Surprise!" they shouted.

After I regained my sight I found myself surrounded by the smiling faces of my friends carrying bags full of steaming takeout. Each person assaulted me with hugs and kisses, not allowing me to escape and taking full advantage of my disoriented state.

"You look cute in my shirt," David teased, and I slapped him away.

"What are you guys doing here?"

David rubbed my head, messing up my hair. "I just couldn't let my little buddy suffer alone!"

"Yeah," added Eileen as she sat on her haunches, smiling and resting a hand on my forehead to check my temperature. "What kind of friends would we be if we didn't come and visit you?"

"What are you wearing?" I asked, noticing her angel wings and halo, and Tobey's antennae.

"Tobey suggested we all wear costumes, for some reason..." Lucy said, showing off her superhero cape. "He bought all of us costumes."

"Why?"

Tobey shrugged. "Why not? Here, I even got one for you." He threw a blue scrap of cloth at me (which I failed to catch), and turning it around in my hands I discovered that it was Heavy Doorah's mask!

"Yo! Thanks man!" I hurriedly shoved it over my head, and felt the power of the world's greatest wrestler surge through me. I brought a weak arm up and used all of my energy to pathetically flex, but David cheered enthusiastically.

"You look like the big man himself!" He grinned.

"You never shut up about HD, and it was on discount so... enjoy," Tobey said with a shrug and a nonchalant smile. I could tell he had gone through a lot more trouble than that to get it. He was just that kind of guy.

Behind them I heard the clattering of plates in the kitchen as Nina and Apronas prepared the food, meanwhile Tobey reached into a bag and retrieved a set of DVD's.

"Which one do you wanna watch first?" he asked.

"Uh, got any on VHS?" I said, and they all began laughing.

"Nina was right! He does live in the dark ages!" Eileen giggled.

Soon enough we were all sitting around the coffee table, eating Otellan Beef and watching 'Dangerous Accoutrements' on a DVD player Nina had brought over. The movie itself was pretty crap, with cheap sets and cheesy dialogue, but the company I had more than made up for it. I found myself sitting at the back, smiling along with my friends and laughing so hard at the jokes Tobey made that it hurt my stitches.

"-And that's why my cousin collects Armadillos, how did you think he got so rich?" David chuckled and slapped his knee.

"Not by milking them!" Eileen's giggle violently turned into a cackle.

David's story had started on how his uncle and father had a joint business venture focused on bringing maid cafes and fishing together (which I think is a pretty neat idea, mind you) but somehow it had ended here. I guess I'd stopped paying attention halfway through but still...

Just what kind of life was his family living?

"It's true." Tobey nodded. "I read a report on international armadillo milk sales and revenue expectancies in a stock and bonds magazine a few months ago. His cousin's company was top of the list."

"There's a list?" Apronas roared, slapping the ground as she fought for air. Her cat ear headband wobbled dangerously, and the cat nose mask she wore made her look pretty goofy.

"Why do you know that?" I asked.

"Because I know things." He winked. "But speaking of lists..." He smiled nefariously at Apronas then addressed us all with open arms as if he was a stage presenter. "Our friend Apronas here has made it onto many lists! Which lists, you may be wondering... Well, some lists as prestigious as 'Urlou's most influential Pop-Idols!'"

Nina gasped, turning to Apronas with her mouth wide open. "No... way..."

Apronas leapt to her feet and pinched Tobey's ear. "You *katsudor de cabritis! Ay!* I should have known... you with your big nose!"

"What does my nose have to do with anything!" Tobey laughed. And winced.

"You are good at the sniffing of clues!"

After he managed to free himself from her grasp he revealed to us a magazine he had found, one with Apronas posing on the front cover wearing a full-on pop icon ensemble of a poofy pink dress, angel wings, a sparkling tiara, and... fishnet gloves.

Oh my.

Now *this* explains a lot.

But it also raises more questions.

"*Asteri Astrella*..." Lucy read, "what does that mean?"

Apronas's death glare faltered and she sat down again. "It translates roughly to... 'Your Star,'" she sighed.

"Aww, that's so cute!" Nina and Eileen squealed in unison.

"It makes so much sense now, the way you act... so sophisticated! I never would have guessed you were famous!" Nina said.

"How did you find this out?" The question had been directed to Tobey who shrugged.

"Since we first met I always thought you looked familiar, so I followed some leads but turned up nothing. Eventually I asked my mother and she said she recognized you. No matter how hard you try to hide your true identity, there is only ever one truth," he said with a wink.

Nina hit his arm and he winced. "Don't say that like you actually did any detective work!"

"I asked witnesses, it doesn't get any more detective-y than that."

"He has a point!" David slapped his back, almost winding the poor boy.

"But, that's not all!" Tobey coughed, and once more he clambered to his feet. "I also managed to get my hands on a copy of her live performance of *'My dear, for you I send kisses'*!" He turned around to search through the pile of DVD's he'd brought but Apronas approached him from behind, her cat ears wobbling.

"Not so fast, alien boy!" she shouted and grabbed the back of his shirt, then with a perfect hip twist and leg sweep combo she threw him to the floor. Since when did pop-idols get hand-to-hand combat training? "We are *not* watching that!"

"Whu?" He exclaimed as he fell, surprise etched onto his face. The two began wrestling and rolling across the floor, battling for supremacy. The entire time he was reaching for the DVD case, and though Apronas got him into armbar after headlock after leg pin, he kept fighting, so she did the last thing she could and sat on him.

"Goddesses... is this how I die...?" he gasped as his skull was crushed, a lone tear escaped his eye. "Thank you..."

The smile I'd been holding had begun to make my face ache, but for that I was glad.

"You gotta be careful now that we know you're famous!" David said with too happy a tone. "Don't go down to the beach alone!"

Apronas looked at him, still sat atop Tobey's head. "Why you say that?"

"Because of Dead Star Cove."

"David!" Eileen shouted, slapping his chest. "Don't scare the poor girl!"

"Why? What is this Dead Star cove?"

"Ooh, ooh, can I explain this one?" Lucy piped up, clapping her hands.

We all looked at her and her clapping slowed.

"Go ahead." David gestured.

"Okay! So, get this," she said, turning to Apronas. "So, about forty or fifty years ago every time a famous movie star would come here they would mysteriously turn up dead at the Cove at the north of the beach. Nobody caught the killer even though it happened for years, and though he hasn't struck for decades there's a superstition that coming here brings terrible misfortune, so famous people usually avoid coming here."

Apronas should have looked scared, but instead she seemed intrigued. "Interesting..." she mumbled. Tobey was still struggling beneath her. "So I will die?"

"I hope not!" Lucy exclaimed, grabbing her hands. "Do *not* be afraid, okay? No killers live here."

"Then explain the slasher." Eileen grunted.

My smile faltered.

"So Nina," David asked with a grin, interrupting the conversation. "Are we going to give it to him or what?" He nodded his head towards me.

"Of course, I'll go get it," she replied, leaving me to wonder what they were talking about. She rummaged through her bag and eventually turned around with a large box wrapped with a bow in her arms. On the side was a familiar insignia of a fork and a rose, and I instantly found myself in disbelief. Even as Nina was handing me the box I was already eagerly tearing through the packaging to find the Miss. Morina Winslow Retro Tea Set I had seen on TV the previous week.

"No way..." I gawked, "this is... fantastic!"

Everyone laughed at my sheer excitement for a tea set, except for Nina who crouched beside me and gave me a smile, placing a hand on my knee.

"I saw it on TV last week and I knew you would want it. And I think being stabbed is probably a good enough reason to ignore the price tag." She winked. "Besides, everyone chipped in."

I carefully extracted each delicate piece to carefully examine it, smiling with deep satisfaction and admiring the fine detailing painted with a gorgeous blue. It even came with its own whisk and mixing bowl! For this, I'd get stabbed *twice*.

"When she first suggested it I thought she was just trying to score a free teapot." David laughed, clumsily turning a cup in his hands. The callousness of the action caused me to cringe, but I kept my mouth shut.

"Don't worry," Tobey said, patting his shoulder. "Even for me this is an odd fascination.

"You guys just don't get it," I tutted, shaking my head. "This tea set is the perfect balance between beautiful and utilitarian. It is equal parts form and function." I rubbed a loving and gentle hand across the bulbous side of the teapot. "This was not only designed to be a treat for the eyes but to perfectly enhance and distribute the flavor of the tea leaves throughout the water by utilizing the perfectly round shape of his body."

I looked up to see each person holding a blank stare.

"I'll demonstrate it for you guys."

I retreated to the kitchen with the box and a collective of eager claps heralded my exit. Setting the pot to boil on the stove I got the powdered leaves ready by whisking them in the little mixing bowl that had been packed in with the set. Tobey watched, somewhat interested in the process, as I got each teacup ready. I told him the step-by-step instructions as I moved from piece to piece, but as I reached up to open the cupboards my body seized up and a hot burning sensation squeezed me. I doubled over gasping, clutching at my side. There was a hand on my back.

"You alright there, buddy?"

My face was screwed up, but I knew that I'd be fine. "Yeah.." I wheezed. I heard him open the cupboard and grab the tin of sugarcubes then set them down on the counter for me. I made sure to breathe calmly in a rhythm I'd learnt when running, and slowly I straightened up.

"Let me check your stitches," Tobey said, and begrudgingly I lifted my shirt.

"There's no bleeding, it seems everything is fine." He poked at my side and I tried not to hiss in pain. "You just have to remember to move slowly."

"I'll try."

"Why do you like tea so much?" he asked, and I shrugged.

"I dunno. So much of our heritage and culture has been lost to time, especially the wars, and while I do wish I was more in tune with my heritage this is the one thing that I can truly connect with. I'm not gonna pick up a blade and become a master, but I can at least learn how to make tea."

"Alright then, Tea-master, what's next in the process?" he asked, humoring me. The pot began to bubble and boil so I took it off the stove and showed him the correct ratio of water to tea powder, and how to mix them together.

Tobey helped me carry the tea on a tray into the living room where everybody gave a collective 'Ooooooh" as they saw their beverages approaching. I poured into the cups, replicating the traditional hand placements as I had seen on TV, and I urged everyone to add milk, honey, or sugar as they desired, as I knew the green tea was an acquired taste. I demonstrated how to pick up the cup and the proper way to enjoy the tea, and then watched intently as everyone copied my movements, scanning each and every face as they smelled the sweet aroma and took their first sip.

"Wow, this is delicious! You should make this more often!" Nina said.

"I wish I could make tea this good," Eileen said.

"I think this is the one thing you're good at." Tobey nodded.

"This is... amazing, please show me how to make it!" Lucy cheered.

"What an unmanly talent..." Apronas scoffed.

"I have to admit you make a good drink," David said, having finished his in one gulp. After listening to their reviews I sat and sipped my own and honestly, I impressed myself.

Chapter Thirteen
"Like stars."

I felt a finger poke at my ribs.

"Wakey wakey." David's smiling face was inches from mine.

"Get lost, stench breath." I pulled my covers up and shoved my head deeper into the couch, screwing my eyes shut and fighting against the warm light of the morning sun.

"Hurtful," he said and retreated.

"Come on sleepyhead, breakfast is almost ready!" Nina called out from the kitchen, inviting my ears to hear the sizzling of food on hot pans. I groaned and sat up. I could feel my hair sticking up in odd directions. I probably looked like Nina.

"You look terrible," Apronas said plainly from where she was perched atop my coffee table eating a bowl of cereal. She stared at me as if I were an interesting game show or something. She was still wearing the cat ears.

"You try getting stabbed," I muttered as I sat up, wary of how much I stretched. David was standing with his hands on his hips as he looked me up and down.

"Feeling any better, sport?"

"Not much. What time is it?"

Everyone scrambled to look for a clock or a watch but Tobey just called out: 'Ten thirty' without even looking up from his morning paper. Everyone agreed, unnerved at his accuracy.

"Why'd you wake me up so early?" I complained.

Nina walked into the room with a plate full of food and placed it into my lap. Bacon and eggs with toast; a staple meal of the morning... for the Elennarians, maybe. "You fell asleep first, and got more hours than most of us, so don't complain!"

Thinking back, the last thing I remembered was Apronas singing after we'd all pressured her into it by chanting for what seemed like hours. Her voice was like the waves softly moving across the sand. I could see why she was so popular back home. "You didn't draw on my face or anything did you?"

"I wanted to, but they wouldn't let me." Tobey sipped at his coffee.

"I was on his side," Lucy said with a grin.

"Thanks," I muttered as I stabbed at a piece of bacon with my fork. It was good. *Damn* good. Why hadn't we adopted this as our national breakfast yet? Maybe 'cause rice was easier to cook. Who knows.

"So when are you guys going to leave?" I asked after having finished breakfast and watched some TV. I tried to flick over to a Miss. Morina Winslow infomercial but Apronas scolded me and turned it back to the sports game she and David had been watching. I guess 'my house my rules' didn't apply here.

"When we all go to the fireworks festival tonight. Don't tell me you forgot." Nina said from behind the couch. She had dragged a chair from the kitchen and set up shop behind me as Lucy and Eileen had taken residence on the other seats. David and Apronas were on the floor and Tobey was sitting by the open door to the balcony, reading his paper. I think this was the fullest my house had ever been.

"When exactly did I agree to this?"

"Last night."

"When, last night?"

"I think it was when we were all getting ready to go to sleep. You oughta get more blankets, it was a good thing we brought our own."

"I was asleep! This must be illegal somehow!"

She flicked my ear. "Illegal or not, you agreed. And it'll be nice to go out anyway."

"Alright, fine. Where are my antibiotics?"

"Where'd you leave them?" Lucy asked.

"In the bag of crap I brought from the hospital."

"Right here," Apronas said, retrieving the little bottle from the plastic bag and throwing it my way. I didn't want to move too fast trying to catch it and tear my stitches, so I just let it whack into my face which of course earned a round of laughter. Some friends I had, I sighed.

"No way..." David exclaimed, and leaned forward, dusting off my Dad's console. "I haven't seen one of these in ages. Does it still work?"

"Sure does. The games for it are in the cabinet over there."

Immediately he scrambled over to it and flung the door open, reading the titles faster than I thought he *could* read.

"Dude... no way." He pulled out the case for 'King of Iron Fist' and his hands trembled. His eyes were as wide as Mr. Washy's as he stared at it. "Can we play it, please?"

"Go right ahead man."

"Awesome!" He dropped to his knees and frantically swapped the disc, and like an excited little kid he watched as the logo for the console came up on screen with its own unique soundtrack. "This is amazing..." he said under his breath, mesmerized by the colours on-screen. Apronas scowled at him for having changed the input.

"Careful, this guy's a champion at that game," Nina said, flicking a thumb my way.

"Oh yeah? I'll just have to show him my might!" He flexed his bicep.

He lost thirty-six times in a row.

"This power... impossible..." His voice was hollow, and his eyes now stared lifeless at the floor. "Impossible."

"I told you," Nina giggled.

No one else wanted to face me but Tobey, who was also put to shame. I had fun watching the rest of them battle, though. They came up with their own tournament and eventually the last two in the running were Nina and David. The tension from the last few fights had only gotten more oppressive, and the excitement more intoxicating. We all cheered and despaired over our chosen hero.

"Go Nina, go! Use the Liebewave beam!" I shouted.

"I'm trying!" she shrieked, furiously mashing the buttons on the controller, trying and failing to input the specific button combo and letting David score free hits as she flailed helplessly.

Her health bar was draining, hit by hit.

Eileen had fallen at the first hurdle and was now cheering David on. Sitting on her knees beside him she crushed the pillow in her arms to within an inch of its life as she stared at the screen with eyes the size of saucers. "Beat her! You can do it David!"

"Where the hell did she get so good?" David cried out as Nina unleashed a ten-hit combo on him, then, in a turn none of us saw coming, he managed to block the sixth and put her on the defensive, unleashing his character's Fists of Fury. I gritted my teeth and Lucy gasped, but Apronas, Eileen and Tobey cheered (Tobey wasn't on anybody's side. He just cheered for whoever was winning at the time).

"Duck, duck!" I yelled and Nina did just in time, releasing an uppercut I'd been on the receiving end more times I could count, then launching a combo that could juggle him for half a minute straight. It had been her only respite against me a few times. I sighed in relief and watched as David lost more and more health with every frame of attack until he countered, threw a punch, got countered, and Nina's leg sweep defeated him.

"Die!" she screamed.

"Player One: Victory!" The game declared, and David threw a palm to his head while Nina cheered and ran over to me, throwing both her hands up for a high-five.

"How'd I do?" She clutched my hands and jumped with glee.

I laughed and felt a surge of pride within my chest. "You did great!"

"What did you think of that last combo? I could barely remember it but my fingers did, by the Goddess that was close."

"Enough rubbing it in my face," David lamented, "I only lost because I was on the right side of the screen."

"Fine then, face me again... if you think you're good enough."

"Challenge accepted!" He declared with a determined grin.

He lost again.

The sun was getting closer to the horizon and in a desperate attempt to cling on it had stained the sky its signature orange, although it was still a few hours until the fireworks were due to go off. It was harder for me to walk down the roads but they took it slow with me, making sure I was okay. The streets were abuzz with people eager for the fireworks; setting up picnic blankets at their favourite spots or looking for somewhere with a good view. After a few more rounds of 'King of Iron Fist' and a couple races in 'Grand Tour XI,' we all began to feel hunger set in. A discussion was held about where we should eat, and after a fierce battle we boys managed to convince the girls to come to Mr. Kobayashi's Eat-Stay place. So that's where we were headed as a rowdy group of teens chatting and cheering, stumbling along together. I smiled to myself. I had what I'd been looking for. I noticed Eileen taking up the rear with me, face a little red and acting a little reserved.

"Nervous about tonight?" I asked.

"Huh?" She looked up at me, her thoughts interrupted. "No. Loud noises don't scare me really."

"No, not that." I nodded my head towards David who was busy retelling a story about 'that one time in practice when we splashed a bucket of paint on the coach's head and found out he had a pet turtle that stole fingers'. Her face went red and she stammered.

"I-I don't know w-what you're talking about."

"Oh Eileen, you think me a fool? I have figured out what the ruse of that letter-"

"Shhh! Be quiet!" she hissed.

"Sorry," I chuckled weakly, but luckily David was too caught up in his storytelling to hear us. "I figured it out. How long have you, y'know, *liked* him?"

"Since last year... The first day of highschool, really. I was really lost because I'd memorized a map of the school that was out of date, and I was starting to panic because I was late for my first class but David showed me where my homeroom was. I'd be totally lost without him."

Ah, that's right. Eileen went to the East Elementary school.

"What're you guys talking about?" David interrupted, and Eileen wailed in surprise.

"Just how we all met." I quickly stated and he nodded, satisfied.

"First day of school, you were lost. I remember," he said with a grin. "We started hanging out with you not long after, right?"

"At the ass-end of that year, actually," I said, shaking my head. "Last term."

"Oh, it seems like we've been hanging out for way longer."

"Maybe that's because you've known me since middle school."

He chuckled. "Okay then, I guess it's only been half a year since I started liking you."

"What do you mean?" Eileen asked, confused.

"I was a bit of a jerk," I weakly chuckled.

"Somehow that's not a surprise," Tobey laughed.

"A bit?" David scoffed a bit too loudly. "This guy here used to be best friends with Oscar."

Great. *Back then*. My favourite topic.

Eileen stared at me with her mouth wide open. "Really?"

"Yeah, when we were kids."

"Wow. I never would have guessed. How long were you friends?"

"Since childhood, really. I moved here when I was pretty young and he was the first person to actually talk to me. Even when we were kids he was a cryptic weirdo, but I needed the company."

"You were also friends with O–" David started but Nina shushed him, placing a hand on his shoulder and placing a finger over her mouth. I appreciated the concern. I really didn't want to talk about this but I didn't want to make it obvious. Eileen didn't catch that though.

"Why aren't you friends anymore?"

"We uh, had some..." How to put this politely? How to put this *at all?* "We disagreed on some things." I finally decided to say, and she nodded to herself.

"Who is Oscar?" Apronas asked aloud.

"A jerk."

"A creep."

"No one you want to know."

Apronas laughed loudly, and threw her head back. "Now I *really* want to meet him!"

We all desperately tried to convince her that *she really didn't,* all the way to the front door of Mr. Kobayashi's refined and unique establishment. Stepping inside, I watched as the girl's faces widened in the same wonder I felt when I'd first arrived, gawking in awe and appreciating all the decades-old decorations hanging on the walls. Apronas looked doubly curious, and we had to explain to her what most of it was, or what it meant, or where it was from. Mr. Kobayashi waved at all of us with an excitement that made me feel right at home, and the Moaning Christmas Man was sitting where I'd last seen him, crooning to an audience that would really appreciate his taste in music come the cold season.

"So what did you order for us?" Lucy asked as she hung her purse on her chair. We had been allowed to use one of the larger tables at the back, although that also meant we were closer to the Moaning Christmas Man.

"Trust me," David said.

"Trust him," Tobey and I echoed.

"...alright then," she conceded, and any further questions were put on delay.

Nina placed her hand on my knee and leaned in to whisper. "*Is he staring at us?*" Her words were uttered with a well-placed fear, and she shuddered at the sight of the man singing.

"*Yes. Don't look directly at him. He can smell your fear.*"

"*Why the hell did you guys bring us here?*"

"*The food is worth it, I promise.*"

"*Doesn't he know what month it is?*"

"*I doubt it. I don't think he knows how to sing either.*" I looked up and he winked at me.

I could feel my soul crap its pants.

"What is this place?" Apronas asked, still in utter disbelief.

"This is what's called a 'Stay-Drink' place. These types of establishments were quite common all throughout this country's historical culture, and were mostly utilized by the working class male after a day of hard work. Married men came here for the relaxing atmosphere and to unwind before they went home, and men who were still yet to marry could enjoy a cooked meal here. These days it is an establishment enjoyed by both sexes," Tobey said with a nod. You could certainly count on him to say more than what was needed.

"Is this a *brothel?*" Apronas hissed, looking around in a panic.

"What? How did you come to that conclusion?" Lucy laughed.

"He was talking about the *sexes*, what is the age of consent in this country?"

We all shook our heads and smiled.

"You've got the wrong idea..." Nina started her explanation but as the miscommunication led her further down the rabbit hole of stammered clarifications and burning cheeks we could do nothing but laugh. It turned out Tobey wouldn't be the only victim of Apronas's tendency to get the wrong message.

With explanations explained and our hunger more than quenched, we decided to pay the tab and head back up the hill to a park near my house to watch the fireworks. The clock was ticking and my crew were beginning to get anxious in their eager anticipation of the explosions. I wasn't as pumped as they were as I'd already seen them before, although it had mostly been through the window while I was watching TV. I had to admit that their excitement was starting to become contagious, but then again I could have just been happy seeing my friends happy.

The park wasn't as full as some of the other places we'd passed by, but I think that's because no one wanted to climb this far up the hill. Even I was starting to regret it, but David picked me up and with me on his shoulders hiked up like a man. I swore Eileen swooned just like the love interest from a black and white movie. Speaking of, I'd noticed she was quieter than usual, probably due to her promise to confess during the festival. We were nowhere near the main fare so I wonder what David thought. Did he think his secret admirer was following us, ready to leap out the dark alleyways to confess? Did he think he was going to completely bypass them? Or had he completely forgotten? I didn't want to ask and put even more pressure on Eileen so I kept quiet.

I looked down and saw a blonde head skipping alongside the crowd.

"Lucy?"

"Yes?" she answered, looking up at me.

"Why are you hanging out with us?"

My question took her by surprise and she lightly shook her head from side to side as she looked for an answer.

"Uh, why are you asking me this?"

"Well, you've got those other friends, right? Why aren't you with them, or Akera?"

"I invited Akera to join us but she said she was busy with something, and you... you were there for me!" she exclaimed with red cheeks. "That's why I'm here... You've been a good friend to me, so it's only fair if I return the favour."

"That's fair enough." I nodded, satisfied with her answer.

"Stop moving so much!" David complained and I laughed, only to make him complain even more. "Why am I still carrying you anyway? Get down!" he shouted and I laughed again as he struggled to bend over and drop me without injuring me. "That's a lot better," he groaned, rubbing his shoulders. "You're not that heavy, but that hike was killer."

"I'm surprised you could carry me that far."

"What, you're saying I look weak sauce or something?"

"N-no, not at all!" I raised my hands as he glowered at me. "I'm just impressed, that's all!"

"Oh!" His smile quickly returned to his face. "Of course! I thought you were gonna try to arm wrestle me or something."

"Calm down big guy, I think you'd beat us all," Tobey laughed.

"Hey David, could I... could I have a word with you, please?" Eileen said, having appeared out of thin air right behind him.

He looked at me like a deer in headlights. "Uh oh, what did I do now...?" he sighed, turning away and following her.

I shook my head with a grin and tried to watch as she got him alone. By then the park had gotten a little more crowded, with a hundred or more people standing in their own little groups of friends and families, so I lost sight of them pretty quickly. Music began blaring over the loudspeakers spread across town which were usually reserved for weather warnings, alerting everyone that the fireworks would be going off soon. The volume of the chatting crowds became hushed, and excited whispers spread like wildfire. Everyone's faces stared at the sky and the stars above, and silence fell over the town until the first firework went off in a bright red explosion.

A roaring boom that shook my bones.

Everyone cheered as more and more were shot into the air with a shrieking whistle before exploding into stardust with a deafening blast. Even I was transfixed. I was never one for fireworks so I'd been inside when it happened for the most part. Except for, well... two years ago, but that's unimportant. This must be why everyone was so excited. I felt like a little kid again, lost in the bright lights of the roaring explosions with my sister by my side holding an apple toffee.

I looked down in trance, and saw Nina silhouetted against the supernovas, dancing. Spinning in a circle with her hair flowing in the wind. She was grinning wildly and her eyes were closed. The light peeked around the soft edges of her face, and her hair glowed like fire. Time paused, but she kept moving. No, time hadn't paused, that's wrong. It's just that no one else existed anymore. No one but Nina.

I stepped forward without even thinking, and like I was in slow motion I went to her. But she didn't stop. She kept spinning, and grinning, and by the goddesses, I'd never felt like this before. No, wait, I had, but this... not like *this*. I somehow found myself right beside her and when she came to a stop her smile grew wider as she saw me there, and she grabbed my hands, sending electricity shooting through my body that set alight every cell that was me.

"It's beautiful, isn't it?" she said and skipped in a circle around me. The world was a blur, occasionally doused in the hues of the rainbow, but she was clear.

"...beautiful..." I mumbled, but she didn't hear me. Suddenly she came to a stop, breathless. Her hair was ragged and wild, she looked like she was either about to cry or fall asleep, her eyes a forest floor stared at mine and she smiled so wide her freckles made new constellations. I thought of kissing her. Of holding her face with my hands and staring into her tired eyes. I imagined the way her voice would weakly escape her lips as she said; *'I love you.'*

I was going to kiss her.

But I didn't.

Why didn't I?

Deep down, I knew.

I made up some lame excuse about forgetting something and quickly rushed away as Nina called my name repeatedly, begging me to stay. Why didn't I stay? Why didn't I stay, dammit!? What the hell was wrong with me? Tell me you idiot, tell me! Why?

Picture a man with a baseball bat.

I bumped into Apronas who practically sneered at me.

"You know I don't like you, right? Don't go confessing to me."

"I wasn't planning on it," I snapped and tried to walk past but she blocked my path.

"You're a liar, Oenos." She spat, the usual warmth associated with that misnomer replaced with searing venom.

What?

"You're lying to yourself," she continued, jabbing a finger into my chest and making my entire body tense in pain. "I know you are stupid, but you're not too stupid enough to not know she likes you too, why are you lying?"

"I'm not lying!"

"Yes you are!" She jabbed me again and the sneer became a snarl. "I spend so much of *my* time trying to make her jealous so that she will say she likes you, but when you are so close you run away! You are lying to yourself and you are lying to her, why? Do you want to hurt her?"

I pushed her hand away.

"There's... there's something I need to do, okay?"

She muttered to herself in her mother tongue, nothing nice I would guess.

Nina, I'm sorry.

I just need a little time.

Chapter Fourteen

"An echo of summer memories."

I faced the window opposite my bed, watching as the curtains softly moved with the wind, accented by the pale moon beyond. It was quiet after the fireworks stopped. It was silent. Nina had called my phone a dozen times but I didn't answer. I couldn't tear my eyes away from the window in case I missed her. I thought of Cicadas. Heat. A gun. A lighter. Smoke. Laughter. A butterfly in a box. Rain. A baseball bat. An evil little flower. But mostly I thought of a girl with pale skin, copper hair, and eyes the colour of a bleeding umbrella.

The evil little seed she'd planted in the middle of my skull with a baseball bat so deeply it hid in the spaces between anything had died long ago. My head still bore the scar of when she'd planted it, and my heart was covered in the millions of words she'd whispered to me, of the kisses she'd given me in secret, of the glances she'd stolen in the middle of class. It had been ruined, and it had been hers. It had been hers for a long, long time even though it had been two years since she had last spoken to me. Since I had last heard her say my name. It had been just as long since I'd seen her look at me and actually *see* me. While my body shuddered and my heart seized every time I'd been in the same room or hallway as her, I wanted nothing more than for her to walk over to me and call me stupid. To call me an idiot. To call me *meat*. Heck, she could whack a baseball bat into the back of my head as hard as she could and I would thank her. I would wish upon every shooting star for the rest of my life for her to quietly reach out and hold my hand to make sure she didn't disappear just *one* more time, to grab me by the tie and mash her face into mine again, to whip a can of soda at me so hard that it made my arms welt up. I would stomp my foot into a million bear traps right here right now if it meant she'd appear before me and spit on the floor between us with a scowl. But Oscar was right.

Life isn't like the movies. There is no happy ending and the credits don't roll, it just keeps going on and on.

I waited, but she never came.

I think I'd been in love with a ghost the whole time.

Chapter Fifteen

"An evil little flower."

I jumped in fright, jolting violently as I was suddenly brought to consciousness by my ringing phone. Immediately my eyes darted to the window though it revealed nothing but darkness and rain. I sighed and flipped my phone open to see the time and who was calling. When did I fall asleep? I had apparently just slept through a whole day sitting propped up against the wall. My back was stiff.

I answered the call.

"Yeah?"

"Oh thank the Godesses you answered!" Lucy cried, and I jumped again. Her voice was raw, like she'd been screaming for hours. "I didn't know who else to call... Oh Goddess... I called the police but they didn't know what to do!"

"What happened?"

"It's Akera!" she shouted, and my blood ran cold.

Today is Sunday.

"What happened to her, is she okay?"

"I don't know..." Lucy sobbed, "she wouldn't answer her phone so I went to her house but it's been completely trashed and... she's missing. I think something happened to her."

I felt my blood turn from ice to molten lava and every inch of my body turned to fire. I knew *who* was responsible, but I didn't know *where*. "Lucy, do you know someone called Dan?"

"Yes I do..." she sobbed.

"Do you know where he lives?"

"No, I don't know where he lives... we would always meet him at a warehouse in the south part of town. It's on Mirrow Avenue, I think."

"Lucy, I want you to call the police and ask for Senior Detective Laine. Tell her to go to Dan's warehouse, but *only* in an hour's time, no sooner than that. And don't mention my name, at all. "

"O-okay, why?"

I didn't answer.

I didn't need to Pause to find Dan's warehouse, but I kept time halted just in case. I was familiar with the southern side of town as I'd run across its streets as a kid and I'd tagged on the underside of the bridge and jumped in its marshes. I'd stolen from the hardware store and destroyed a classroom just for fun. It was my home, and I was its king. At least, I used to be.

Not even Oscar still held that crown.

We really weren't kids anymore.

Down an overgrown road with potholes and discarded cans I found Dan and his goons. Their popped-collars and lack of ties made it obvious who they were. They were idiots who tried to play cool by looking careless, but really it did nothing to hide the fact that they were human scum. Their warehouse door was wide open and they milled around aimlessly. They didn't care. Nobody was coming for them.

Nobody but me.

I stomped towards them through the pouring rain, and the first guy who noticed me approached me with his hands outstretched.

I paused time and sent a fist into his face that broke his sunglasses in two.

As time continued he dropped backwards like a bag of bricks, clutching his nose and crying out in a mixture of pain and surprise. The rest of them looked over in alarm and saw me standing above him. They couldn't see my face out in the dark, but they saw a clear threat.

"Woah, what the hell!? Who are you?" the second one shouted as he rushed me. I punched him in the back of the head and he dropped to the floor, unconscious. The whole gang began shouting then, and all eyes were on me. I had interrupted Dan's card game and I saw him sneer. *He had no idea who he was dealing with.*

One by one they came out to try and fight me but they never saw my fists coming. Some were fast, but I was faster. Some swung pipes but their choice of weaponry didn't matter; they couldn't touch me. I was a god compared to them. A few would get back to their feet, but no matter how many times they got up they would never get close. There were maybe thirteen writhing bodies by the time the assault was over and I hadn't gotten hit *once*.

An evil little flower sprouted in the centre of my forehead as I stomped on a few of them to make sure they'd stay down.

The whole time Dan had remained inside, ordering his goons to try and stop me. He'd even tried to slink away while I was busy but I sealed the back door with barrels and drums, and there was no way in hell he was getting away.

For me minutes passed, but for him every light and every window exploded at once. The liquor bottle with a rag set alight and shoved in the neck that someone had thrown at me had inexplicably landed on a stack of boxes housing their drugs, setting it all alight. All they had was slowly turning to ash. The only thing left that was casting any light at all was the TV, now playing nothing but static. Dan covered himself as hundreds of shards rained upon him, and he spun to face the TV with wide eyes. I laughed from every direction but waited until he turned back to me before throwing a punch into his face. I *wanted* him to see me coming.

He finished stumbling and came at me, fast, readying a punch. All I had to do was pause time and lean to one side, and his fist went flying past. In my rage I threw my skull into his and my head exploded into stars and pain, I was so dazed I didn't see the punch he sent into my jaw coming. His fist was like a piston and my brain rattled around in my skull as I limped backwards.

"You're a fast one," he grinned, his confidence renewed. He sauntered over to me with a cocky attitude I had to punish him for, and I easily ducked under his next punch, giving him one in the stomach that made him double over and another that arced upwards and into his grimacing face. He lurched backwards, unable to defend against an unending attack targeting his ribs, his face, his sides. I couldn't help but laugh as he cried out in fear and I grabbed his ear, wrenching it to the side, and as he hissed he exposed his neck which I sent a snaking fist into. He fell to one knee as he coughed violently, gasping desperately for air. This feels *good,* I thought with a grin as I watched his arm knock everything on the table to the floor in his desperate search for a weapon. I took a baseball bat from one of his fallen soldiers and his eyes widened as I pulled it out from behind my back. *Magic trick.* I held it out and he snatched it so tightly his knuckles went white, and he swung it blindly, screaming.

"How the hell are you doing that!?" he cried in disbelief as none of his swings made contact. I stood still for long enough for him to actually swing it *at* me, and I simply paused time and took it out of his hands. Swinging it at his head and resuming time halfway through I listened to the crunch of the bat making contact with the bone, with a grin on my face. He fell against the table and I swung it against his back and he howled, then I swung it against the back of his leg and he crumpled to the floor.

The evil little flower was in full bloom, watching in anticipation as I unleashed hell upon this poor soul surrounded by its flames, and it listened as I laughed, unhinged, raising the bat above my head for the next swing. The edges of me became blurred and my face was gone, nothing but static. I was a medium, talking to the dead past. I was going to break his legs into a million pieces. He was never going to run again. I swung it down.

But I stopped myself.

I wouldn't do that.

I'm not like Oscar.

I'm *nothing* like Oscar.

Then why are you enjoying yourself so much?

Dan grabbed a bottle and smashed it, spinning around to swing its jagged edge wildly at me. I didn't even pause time as I swung the bat and wrecked his hand, shattering his bones as the bottle broke in his grip, slicing his palms open and digging their way through the meat of his fingers. He fell to his knees gasping and crying and clutching at his hand as it poured blood in a steady stream onto the floor.

"Leave. Akera. Alone." I commanded, breathing heavy. Speaking with a stern confidence I'd never had before. The fire raged on behind me, having grown immensely in size. He still couldn't see my face, but I knew he could see my eyes. Staring wide and unblinking. I grinned widely. A demon stood before him. "Leave her alone or it'll be your other hand too. And your legs. And your eyes." He looked at me with unabated fear and I leaned in, letting him see my smile. "And I'll enjoy it, too."

The little flower sung my praises, its little voice begging for more, more, *more.* It whispered in my ear to ready the bat, and swing for the fences. *Homerun, homerun.* It chanted, over and over. *Make him look ugly forever.*

I dropped the bat and walked over to the fire extinguisher. I figured that the emergency services could deal with it, but I didn't want to risk anyone's life. Instead I walked over to where Akera lay, still asleep, and I picked her up and carried her out into the still rain.

Dan was already gone.

I'm sure that by now you're well aware that I'm not exactly the most physically capable guy, but I gritted my teeth and struggled through the pain of my screaming muscles and carried Akera all the way to the hospital.

I ended up having to get my stitches resown.

Chapter Sixteen

"Turning point in history."

My alarm went off without any regards as to how I'd feel about its incessant screeching, and I slapped it again and again until it shut up. Slowly, very slowly, I brushed away the cobwebs of my unconscious mind as I prepared for the day ahead. The sun was shining warmly and the sky was an inviting blue, but I didn't care much for its invitation today. I felt like I was the dead walking, fresh from the grave. Nina wasn't waiting at our usual spot, and she hadn't texted me either. Could be that I was later than usual. I sighed and carried on.

There was no one else on the road, no one at all. I wasn't that late, surely? I hadn't even brought my watch to check the time so I ignored the headache seizing my brain and walked on. It was eerily quiet, there weren't even birds singing to break up the silence. I shook the feeling of unease from my spine as best I could. When I finally reached the school gates I finally saw another person and I felt relief wash over me. It was two nobodies I had never seen before, chatting in hushed tones about stolen police weaponry, but I planted a hand on their shoulder and as they looked at me in surprise I said: "Thank the Goddesses for you."

They looked at me as if I was mad.

Limping through the halls I was disturbed to find that no one was crowding the halls. There was no bustling, there was no screaming and cheering and jeering. What the hell? Where was everyone? I was getting seriously sick of the emptiness and I scowled as I wandered the empty school, finding nothing but amber leaves that had snuck through open windows. Eventually my search had taken me outside where I finally, *finally* found people. They were in the gymnasium... oh duh, of *course* they were. It was Athletics appreciation day, wasn't it? It was also that muffin day–no, baking day. I could do with a muffin though. Maybe they'd have a muffin for sale, I thought as I strolled up to the open double doors. Someone stepped out, blocking the way and casting all thoughts of baked goods aside. It was Tobey. I sighed in relief but he wasn't smiling, he wasn't perched in some goofy position trying to make me laugh. His face looked grim as he called me by my name.

"Yes, Tobetobii?"

"I haven't been honest with you," he said.

"About what?"

"I don't have much time to explain so you're going to have to take what I say next at face value. Okay?" I nodded. "The lives of our friends and the future itself depend on what you do next."

I wanted to joke. I wanted to mock him and jab at his ribs, but I was too tired. And even worse was the feeling that he was being serious. *Dead* serious. The air stirred, but nothing else did. Even the people I could see running around in the gym were eerily quiet. They were leaping and cheering, but there was no sound. I could see Nina with a determined look on her face standing in the middle of the court, waiting for the baton to be passed to her.

"I'm not human," Tobey said.

"You aren't what now?"

"I am not human. I have no mother, and I have no father." His tone was strained. I decided not to interrupt anymore. "The world is odder than you might think. When The Godesses created the universe, concepts and cosmic irregularities were birthed at the same time. Some of those Cosmic Gods became Primordial Elders, and one called 'The Entity' created me. It is a singularity of consciousness; it is a being of pure information without form that exists all throughout time on a single plane.

"It has taken upon itself the duty of detailing and compiling all the information of the universe that has ever existed, the current collapsing of infinite possibilities concurrent with the Collective Universe Observation, and all possible futures."

I was struggling to keep up. This was some sort of sick joke, right?

...right?

"The construction of my physical body is similar enough to what you would call a bioroid; a biological organism of artificial creation. I was created with the sole intent of observing humanity and gathering information via the use of social interaction. I am able to manipulate space to a limited degree, but not time. I am able to alter that which does not possess a soul, like my creator before me, but I cannot influence that which has a soul; Thus I come to you with vital information.

"I know you possess the ability to pause time. It's a quirk of your genetic makeup able to manifest due to a genetic inheritance from your elven ancestors. An ability that would make you, in human terms, an Augment. I have known since the day we met that you possessed such capabilities and it is the reason I was given my second objective; to observe you. I also know that currently there are two other people in this localized area who are also able to pause time. During the last few months they have been going through their own story, a mirror to your own that you will never fully know, that you will never learn. You've crossed paths but today marks a turning point in history. Your decision will bring upon the fate of the world. I cannot do anything but give you this warning: There is a very real possibility that people will die. Who, and how many, is an outcome based heavily on your upcoming decision. Whoever dies will be erased from the records by me. I am not able to manipulate matter with a soul... But a corpse does not have a soul."

My hands began to shake. This jerk was screwing with me, wasn't he? This was not the time for one of his stupid jokes, I was really not in the mood. But I somehow felt as if he wasn't. I knew his tells. I knew the way his lip would twitch at the edges when he was trying to hold in laughter. I knew right now that he hadn't changed tone and he was speaking as if this were some stupid fact he'd absorbed and was now regurgitating.

What the hell?

"Why are you telling me this?" I choked.

"Because your influence is a large factor in dictating the future of the universe."

"Why me?"

"Because you are like *them*."

The words choked and died in my throat.

"Right now I am not allowing the transference of soundwaves between the walls of this gymnasium. Each and every student that is not absolutely necessary for this interaction is within these walls, and they will not interfere with the upcoming altercation. However I must warn you. I have created a bubble of repeating synchronicities so that no harm will fall upon the rest of the student body, but it comes with the serious side effect of being able to be altered by powerful emotions."

I wanted to say something, but I was interrupted by the roars of a gun firing. I spun to face the direction I'd heard it and found myself pointed towards the front gates. "You have now entered the sub-inversion reality. They will not be aware of it, although there is a possibility that they could project their delusions into physical matter," Tobey said. "We're depending on you."

Why me?

I limped towards the front gates and found myself showered with rapidly shedding leaves. Each one was a makeshift snowflake; unique in its own way, although they glowed bright fiery red. There were three people at the front gates. Two standing, one on the ground. A police car was sitting behind them with the lights off. I limped closer and found myself facing some people I struggled to recognize as their hair was grey, like ash, but it was dyed, unnatural. Were they trying to imitate my snow-white hair? Was this some sick homage to me? The two members of the committee who I'd helped hang up posters stood side by side and I couldn't tell you if they were lovers, siblings, or... whatever, but with their matching hair they looked like twins. I approached without any sense of urgency and they just stood and waited. Both had a gun in their hand, smoking barrels. Oscar was writhing in pain, gasping for air as the puddle of his blood grew bigger and bigger beneath him, soaking his clothes.

"Life isn't like the movies..." The Boy said, his voice quieter than the wind.

"There is no happy ending," The Girl continued, as if sighing.

"And the credits don't roll."

"It just keeps going on, and on, and on." The Girl's gaze followed a leaf as it danced through the air.

"Isn't that what he always says?" The boy said, and nudged Oscar with his foot.

The two of them were clad in black, with red armbands that had 'God' and 'Goddess' written on them respectively. They both looked tired, or maybe that's how they usually looked. I noticed blood on their sleeves, hidden by the dark material of their clothing. It was too much blood for Tobey to have been their first victim.

I shuddered at the thought.

"The attack on the warehouse last night. Was that you?" The boy asked.

I saw no point in lying.

"Yes. It was. A friend needed my help."

"You didn't kill anyone," said The Girl. It didn't sound like a question.

"You help others. That is what makes you different."

Oscar gasped, and grabbed at leaves.

"Will you help us?"

I didn't have the slightest clue what they wanted from me.

"He was right about one thing." The Boy looked down at Oscar. "This world is rotten. Sink, sink, sinking in its own rust and rot. This town is hell. Everything is meat and rot and it keeps going forever."

I could have sworn that I'd heard that somewhere before.

"We're just as bad as the rot," The Girl sighed, "we're just as stupid. We're just as mentally defective and screwed up as the rest of the rot. We're all just one giant puddle of meat marching forward."

"But what is 'forward' anyway? Where is it? How can we find such a thing?"

"If there is a forward we've been facing the wrong way the whole time."

"Wouldn't it be better if tomorrow didn't come at all?" They said in unison.

Eerie. Just what the hell were they talking about anyway? Why were they speaking in such vague concepts? How smart do they think I am? Using big words and stupid sentences doesn't make you look smart!

Why could I hear a violin?

"Desiring death does nothing but make it harder to accept." The Girl's voice was more firm. As if each sentence they spoke was solidifying their resolve somehow.

"So what if it wasn't suicide?"

"If we fulfill our promise to become more than the labels that have been put on our backs, would that make us evil?"

"If we were to treat the world the way it treated us, would that make us evil?"

"If we were to make the world anew, and make it a kind place. Would *that* make us evil?"

"If a missile were to fly across the sky and we were to ask for happiness from such a thing, would that make us evil?"

"Is the only answer to live everyday facing the wrong direction?"

"To rot, and rust, and go on and on forever facing the wrong direction?"

I was still lost. Nothing they were saying made any sense.

"I don't understand," I said.

A bright beam of light blinded me, and as I turned away I found a blackboard behind me. I was in the way of a projector's beam that now showed the words 'exam time' on the screen. Is this that delusion thing that Tobey had very vaguely mentioned? Turning back around only revealed that I was in some kind of classroom. One where every desk and seat was covered in hundreds of pages of paper with wild scribbling on them. The words 'kill past, kill future' had been written a hundred times on each. The light flashed again and I was blinded for a second.

"We want to kill our past, so we can have a future," The Boy announced, but he was nowhere to be seen. The Girl continued his sentiment. "We want to kill the future, so we can live in the present." I couldn't see her anywhere either.

The projector slide rolled over and now the board held the projected words: 'World Domination is World Destruction'. My silhouette was joined with a boy and a girl standing on either side of me. I turned but they weren't there.

"What the hell does that mean?" I shouted and the projector flashed again, blinding me. When the black spots receded and my eyesight was restored I found myself in an alleyway downtown, the same one where I'd been talking with Lucy. The rain was suspended in midair. How did I get here? Was I still in school and this was only a delusion, or was this the real thing? Looking to my left I saw and heard a massive parade of dancers with fishnet stockings and smiles that were too big doing cartwheels in front of rotund men carrying a band's worth of instruments and playing them all at once. Hundreds of people were dressed in circus garb and swaying from side to side, back and forth. There were whistles and cheers, and I realized they were chanting 'Kill the past, kill the future!'

I heard a flurry of footsteps behind me and I turned just in time to see a shadow flitting past the mouth of the alleyway. '*This seems familiar'* I scoffed, but set off with a limp and followed the silhouette in the rain. Even though time had seemingly been Paused -suspended raindrops and all- the parade kept playing on, revealed to me in slivers peeking between buildings and audible from a mile away. The girl up ahead was wearing her black clothes and her 'Goddess' armband. She looked back at me and grinned. She was awfully pretty, actually. How had I not noticed before?

This is not the time for that.

She ran up a set of stairs and leapt over a railing, dropping somewhere below. I followed along and without looking leapt over, hoping to land on my left leg but looking down I saw nothing but black.

Screaming, I hurtled through a million universes. Neon shining through raindrops. I was falling sideways? I broke through some clotheslines as I fell. Yes. Somehow I was falling sideways.

Could somebody please explain this to me?

In simple terms, please.

When I finally opened my eyes I was safe, on stable ground, surrounded by Nina's garden. I was on the rooftop. When did I...? I really gotta stop asking questions and just go with the flow here. Life is a wave and I've just got to ride it... I think I heard someone say that before.

The only other person on the roof was a girl with long hair as black as the night, accompanied by a cat who was just as dark. They were both standing at the edge of the roof, staring at the track field below. I approached Apronas who stood there looking rather unimpressed with the runners below. I thought I could see myself sprinting within the chalk oval far below.

Apronas sighed. "You know I don't like you, right?"

I nodded. "Yeah, I could've guessed."

"You are so stupid. Such a liar. Nobody could be as stupid as you."

"Thanks."

"Don't thank me, don't even say anything. You shouldn't even be near me. I'm too good for you. You are stupid, and ugly, and I am gorgeous."

The cat meowed in agreement.

"See that boy down there?" She pointed at the boy with white hair running on the track. "*He* is worth something. He is amazing. You are nothing compared to him, *Oenos*."

My feet weren't touching the ground anymore. It had taken me a few moments no notice but I was definitely floating. and I began to elevate faster and faster. By the time I tried to reach out and grab the railing I had already risen too high, and I couldn't do anything but scream as I began flipping over in midair. Apronas and the cat looked on unimpressed as I fell upwards and upwards, higher and higher. Nina had appeared above me, completely massive in scope and size, stretching on for miles and miles and miles. She could have held the world in her hand, and she became everything that ever was. Her tired eyes were full of tears and I screamed as I hurtled towards one at a million miles an hour but she just sobbed my name.

I landed with an explosion of water and desperately I thrashed around and gasped for air only to realize it was a grand total of two feet deep. I was safe. Somewhat.

With a groan I got to my feet. I was in some kind of salt flat. There was nothing for miles, just water and blue skies that melted together, leaving me with no horizon to peer upon.

"Life isn't like the movies, is it?" said a voice. "Psst. Down here!" I looked at my feet and a watery reflection of Oscar grinned at me. "Don't we look kind of similar like this?"

"Don't compliment yourself so much," I said and he laughed.

"What's that!?" he shouted and pointed at the sky, but when I looked there was nothing there. I returned my gaze only for him to leap through the water and throw a fist into my face that sent me reeling.

The water hindered me as I stumbled and lost my footing, but instead of hitting water I hit stairs. Head over heels over head over heels. Bones and meat crashing into every corner of the stairwell until my fall was cushioned by something soft and I came to a stop. My whole body ached, and I groaned as I pulled myself up. I felt something warm and looked down to see blood. *My* blood. Well, blood that belonged to the me lying on the floor with a knife in his back.

This was too much.

This was *far* too much.

What kind of demented vision was I looking at?

Was this Oscar's mind?

Was this... *my* mind?

The pool of blood beneath the me gasping on the floor spread outwards, and he sunk into it. I sunk into it? Whatever, point being, it was warping the world as it expanded and it wasn't going to have me. Well, me again. Whatever!

I turned on my heel and limped as fast as I could but I could hear the walls cracking and splintering behind me, showering me with dust and flecks of paint. There was a window up ahead, at the end of the hallway. If only I could run faster... Faster, faster! If only I could run faster, faster! If only my legs worked! I pushed with all my might and ignored the screaming in my thigh and leapt through the glass, shattering it and colliding with the fire escape outside, catching my ribs on the hard metal railing and gasping for air only to taste smoke.

I found myself in the company of Akera and Lucy Lou who were sharing a cigarette. The world around us was broken, although that might be the wrong word for it. The city was now a sequence of repeating and rolling buildings that rose sideways up out of the ocean that formed a moat around the school, but no... that's wrong. *We* were rising sideways out of the city, as I could feel gravity was trying to pull me down. I held onto the railing for dear life.

"All I do is complain," Akera stated, puffing away at her cigarette and unaffected by gravity. "All I am is rude and uncompassionate."

"Yeah, but you have a good reason to be," I said, "you can learn to be nicer."

"You know I've been hurt by a boy before," Lucy said as she took the cigarette from Akera, and puffed on it just as violently. "I'm broken. I'm used goods."

"That's the silliest thing I've heard you say," I sighed, and gave her a smile.

"It's nothing you haven't thought before." They said in unison, shrugging as the school erupted in an explosion that tore brick from brick and sent me flying through the air as they laughed somewhere behind.

"Bye O-ey!" I heard them giggle.

I fell through the sky, tumbling through the blue blue sky until I crashed into the ground in a cloud of dust and splintering wood. Every inch of my body was in astute amounts of pain but I ignored it, groaned, and sat up anyway, coughing up dust and smoke.

The Twins were in front of me, standing within the husk of the post-explosion school building. I could tell thanks to the desks and chairs scattered across the room that we were in the remains of a classroom on the ground floor. The Boy was standing with his hands in his pockets looking at a broken clock that was precariously hung up on a door frame which was all that remained of a wall. The Girl was sitting in front of me on the other side of a campfire that had been made using textbooks. She looked bored, holding a marshmallow she'd stabbed with her knife above the licking tongues of the fire.

"The conditions of the world we live in are a set of rules completely made up by humanity and government. Once we humans took control we had to create new rules, unnatural ones that disregarded our nature. Laws and rules and grades and taxes and war and culture and romance.

Gone is the human condition, replaced by 'The Human's Conditions,'" I said.

Words not my own had spilled from my mouth.

"Do you think it's better to kill ourselves by living a life we're unhappy with?" said The Boy, as he clicked his fingers the world outside the smoking rubble instantly transformed into blue skies and green fields.

"Or is it better to use our power to destroy the world so *we* can be happy?" The Girl said, clicking her finger and turning everything back to wreckage and ruin.

"What hurts you is often what makes you happy."

"Is it better to suffer, to enjoy, to suffer, to enjoy, in a never-ending cycle that repeats until the day that we all die?"

"No one loves us. No one loves you."

Someone tapped my shoulder and I nearly jumped out of my skin. With a gasp I spun around and came face to face with Nina. Standing behind her was Tobey. David, and Eileen, along with... Otille and my parents.

"Sorry," Nina said, "I don't forgive you for pushing me over. I've always hated you. You have never once made my life better, and the only reason I keep you around is because you can pause time." She waved her red notebook in front of my face. "It's the only thing even remotely interesting about you."

"You've always been a jerk." David shrugged. "That's just who you are."

Eileen looked away. "I don't want to be associated with someone like you."

Otille nudged her glasses up her nose. "I can't stand being near you. Why do you think I moved so far away?"

My mum and my dad grinned widely, like they always did. "We hate you too, son! You're worthless and disgusting and pathetic and we can't stomach the fact you share our genetics!"

Tobey walked forward and crouched in front of me, shaking his head. "I've been observing you for the last year and I must say, you are one pathetic excuse for a human. What a waste of a year."

"This is all fake!" I cried, turning back to the twins. "It's not real!"

"Isn't it?" The Boy asked.

"Then who is the you they love?" The Girl pondered as she removed a terribly charred marshmallow from the fire.

"We know who we are. Who are you?" The boy pointed at a desk in the far corner of the room and a flash of light like you'd see on a stage lit it up, revealing someone taking a nap, resting their head on the top of the table. I recognized the white hair as my own. "Is that you? Are you the pathetic loser who doesn't do anything? Who's lazy and stupid and cynical?"

There was another flash of light on the opposite side of the classroom, revealing another me covered in blood. His white hair was stained red, and he tapped a baseball bat on the floor repeatedly, grinning from ear to ear and staring at me with a deranged look in his eyes. "Or is that you?" The girl asked, "Are you the monster who enjoyed beating helpless gangsters to within an inch of their life?"

They stared at me, waiting for an answer.

"I'm both and neither."

I'm sadder than both, for one.

"Are you avoiding the question?"

"No. Those are individual perceptions of the different aspects that are me."

The Boy raised his hand into the air and snapped his fingers and everything turned dark, as if someone had turned off the lights. The campfire had gone out too, but I could hear the rustle of tree branches swaying gently in the night. I was somewhere deep in a forest in the dead of night. The song of the chirping cicadas was deafening, and my back was absolutely soaked in sweat, it was so hot. Two voices discussing something spoke in turn, one more commanding than the other, deeper within the forest. I crept towards the glow of a campfire and found Oscar and Ophelia standing arm in arm. He was shorter, and she was too, but that wasn't the only difference. Blood spilled out of her mouth had long-since dried on her face and neck. Her front tooth was missing and her eye was black. Oscar was grinning. Her trembling hands held his face, and she stood on her tiptoes to get closer to him. Her eyes closed as their lips got closer and closer...

"Hey, hey!" I shouted, and they turned to face me. "Just what the hell is the meaning of this? Why am I seeing this? Why here and now!?"

Nobody answered.

"What the hell did I possibly do to deserve seeing this again!?"

Oscar slowly strolled over to me whilst Ophelia shook behind him, looking away. He pulled a baseball bat out from behind his back. *Magic trick.*

"Die, meat!" he shouted as he swung it against my head.

There was a crack and I landed roughly on my back with my skull ringing in absolute pain and leaving me seeing double. I could feel the cracks spreading across the bone. There were... many voices... many shapes, moving around... It was like looking out the window of a moving car and just seeing blur and colours, but knowing you're seeing *something.* I shook my head and looked again and I found myself still in the forest, but the parade had returned and they were dancing in a large circle around me. Laughing and grinning and pointing at me. Cheering and jeering and snickering.

Amongst the crowd were two Oscars. One dancing with Ophelia, and another dancing with Nina. Spinning across the dirt and fallen leaves and dipping and diving and spinning and pulling her closer, closer. The moon above opened her eye and stared down at the ritual below, at the chanting, at the dancing, at the flames licking at the dry forest. Oscar twirled Ophelia and held her outstretched, and she fell to the ground limp as he let her go, landing roughly. He approached me, holding his hand out.

"May I have this dance?" Oscar laughed.

"I'm getting real tired of this!" I screamed, and slapped his hand aside. The parade stopped moving. Rain began to fall from overhead in a thick shower like a monsoon. I didn't care who was watching anymore.

"I pulled myself out of that pit you threw me in! I did it! I got myself out! I survived what you put me through and you lost!" I began laughing, tears streaming down my face. I grabbed at Oscar's shirt, blindly pulling him close and screaming into his face so he'd hear what I had to say. "You lost and I won! All the meaning you so desperately needed, all that effort you went through to create meaning for your miserable life was for nothing... you lost."

When I opened my eyes I saw my own face staring back uncomfortably. He/I pushed me off and straightened his bright red school tie. He was Oscar. He was me. I was Oscar. Nina was lying on the ground behind him. Oscar and I are one and the same.

"Let's get it over with then, shall we?" he said, holding up a baseball bat which he swung against my thigh.

I felt the bone snap.

I felt it snap, *again.*

My scream erupted so coarsely I felt it tear my throat into shreds as I grabbed my knee and rolled, gasping in pain. It was deafening. It was encapsulating. Never in my life had I felt so much pain. The bone was stabbing through my leg and there was blood everywhere. It was everywhere. It was the only thing I could focus on. My leg was broken and I'd never run again. I'd have to crawl out of this damn forest, it hurt. Oh Goddesses it hurt.

"Don't give up." A soft sweet voice cut through the agony as a cool hand touched my cheek, calming me in an instant. Even through blurry eyes I didn't recognize the girl. I had never seen her before, but her hair was white like mine. "Don't stop until it's over. You can't keep looking to the past, you have to stake your entire life on the here and now. I believe in you," she said, her smile filled with pure warmth. The pain in my knee completely dissipated and I wasn't even lying down anymore. I was standing in front of the school beneath the two oak trees and Oscar was lying down on the ground in front of me.

Who was she? I looked around to find the white-haired girl but instead I found Oscar and Ophelia standing with a gun to Nina's head.

No, that's wrong, I'm sorry.

I'm still a little confused.

The Boy and The Girl were standing on either side of Ophelia who was holding a letter in her hand. The orange leaves hanging suspended in midair was evidence that time was Paused, along with the fact that Ophelia was very still, which was unlike her.

"We are killing the sorrow of our past," The Girl started.

"So we can have happiness in the future," The Boy finished.

I looked at Ophelia's face. At the constellation of freckles dotting her nose I had imagined a million times. I looked at the scars on her face that I had yet to memorize and the black eye that had never fully healed. Goddesses... She was so beautiful.

The Girl thumbed back the hammer.

"No, stop!" I screamed, and dropped to my knees. Heaving sobs wracked my body. "Please, don't, I'm begging you!"

"Why not?" They asked.

"I spend every night lying awake digging through the scars that failed to heal. What could have been, haunts me. I feel the pain of what I've lost every day. But I know now that I have to let go. Ophelia hurt me, she destroyed me. Oscar did too. I am nothing but ruined. But I learnt to let go... maybe you could do the same."

I looked up, and found that the Girl had lowered her gun.

"You aren't on our side, are you?" she asked.

I looked down.

I took a breath.
I looked back into her eyes.
I shook my head.

Chapter Seventeen

"Responsibility."

When time resumed Ophelia found no one at the front of the school waiting for her except Oscar, who was delirious and gasping in pain. Writhing in a pool of his own blood. Flipping her phone open she thumbed in the three numbers needed to contact the emergency services before stopping herself and considering the situation for a few seconds, then she put her phone back in her pocket and kicked him so she had his attention. He looked up at her with tears in his eyes and she said something I couldn't hear, then she turned and walked away.

The Twins had driven off in their stolen police car and left me crying at her feet, but I ran (well, limped) back towards the gymnasium. I still couldn't hear the roar of the cheering students inside as I arrived, but Tobey was right where I'd left him, and he looked up at me in surprise. Apronas was there too, but she was shouting at him without any volume reaching me.

"That was quick," Tobey remarked as he checked his watch.

"Where's Nina?"

He pointed inside, and I ran in as fast I could, pushing past Apronas who finally seemed to notice me. There was an explosion of sound as I passed through the doorway that threatened to deafen me. The bleachers were filled with hundreds of students cheering on two teams playing volleyball. Nina was among them, and though I wished I could watch her play, there were bigger things than her and I happening at that moment. I stumbled onto the court and everyone began shouting at me to get out of the way.

"Nina!" I shouted, "Nina!"

She looked at me from the opposite side of the net and scowled.

"Nina, you *need* to come with me, right now!"

She pouted. "No I don't."

"Nina, right now, okay, right now! Right now!"

"At least explain yourself."

"It's the Time-Pausers!" I screamed and she looked at me, stunned. The entire hall fell silent. "Hurry up!" I screamed.

"Sorry, please continue without me," she profusely apologized to her teammates. I didn't have the time to wait so I limped on, but she quickly caught up to me. "What's going on!?" she hissed.

"The other Time-Pausers just told me they were going to try to bring utter destruction to the world so they could be happy or something, and there's only one place I can think they could go to do that."

"The... military base?"

"Correct. Also I'm sorry for running away last night. That was not very cool of me. I need to be more forthcoming and honest with my feelings," I said as we marched towards the front gates of the school.

"Is that Oscar!?" Nina shrieked upon seeing him lying in a puddle of blood. He was still breathing, so that was good.

"Yes. Ignore him," I said, and we charged right past.

"Where are we going?" She hurried to keep up with me.

"To the military base."

"Oh, right. How are we getting there?"

I stopped and faced her. There was no other option that I could think of.

"We are going to steal a car."

"What!?" she shrieked, "no way in hell am I doing that!"

"The fate of the world depends on it, Nina! And you're the only person I know who can drive!"

"I *can't* drive! That's why I've failed three driver's tests now!"

I took a deep breath and calmed down. I took a few steps to compose myself, breathing in, and out, slowly. I kept my gaze fixed at the floor, and I stretched, reaching for my feet and picking up a rock. Easing back up I kept controlling my breathing...

And sent a rock through the nearest car's window.

"What the hell was that!" Nina screamed again.

"Shut the hell up and listen!" I shouted and limped back to her. She shrunk away but I grabbed her face in my hands. I stared right into her forest floor eyes.

"Two things. The first is that you're driving that damn car, and the second thing is that I'm in love with you. I am, I really am."

"Oh..." Her face went red. "Really?"

"Well, assuming we can get it started."

"No, you dummy!" she giggled, and pulled my face to hers. A field of flowers in my heart bloomed all at once, sending petals into the air like snow. Electricity and fireworks and anything exciting I'd ever experienced... heck, even that screwy brain-trip I'd just been on didn't come close to this! Nothing could compare to the girl with eyes that always looked tired, and whose hair was always messy, and whose top lip that always looked smudged was smushed against my top lip. Oh Goddess... There was nothing like right here, right now.

Nina pulled herself away from me slowly, and she stared into my eyes, looking from one to the other. Rubbing a thumb across my bottom lip. "I love you too," she said softly, then she kissed the corner of my mouth, then my cheek, then my lips again. "I love you too," she repeated breathlessly, stroking a thumb across my face and burying me in kisses.

I took her hand in mine. "We uh..." My cheeks were red and my heart was hammering inside my chest, trying to break free so it could soar across the sky and into the infinite cosmos. "We should probably save the world..."

"Oh right, that!" She perked up and threw the car door open, leaping inside and climbing over the centre console whilst making sure not to cut herself. I sat down on the glass shards and winced as I felt them poke into my ass. Nina and I desperately searched for the car keys, digging through the glove box, checking the cup holders and throwing loose change into the backseat before finally flicking down the sun blind finding them.

"What luck!" She grinned. "But... what if they Pause?"

Huh. The thought hadn't crossed my mind.

Momentum, right? No, I don't think this applies here. I hadn't tried to Unpause her before, but maybe, *maybe*, if I focused hard enough I would be able to 'kick-start' her, and maybe I could do the same to the car. I would just have to maintain physical contact with both.

"Uh, here hold my hand." I scratched at the back of my head.

"Why?" She blushed.

"I'll try to keep your momentum going..."

"Okay, but this car's a manual."

"What's that supposed to mean?"

"It means I'll have to use both hands to drive. One on the wheel, one on the gearstick. Which means you'll have to..." Her face went red and she looked away. "You'll have to hold onto my thigh."

I cleared my throat. This was for the good of the world.

I put my hand on her thigh.

Nina peeled out of the street with the tires squealing like a wild hog, and suddenly I was fearing for my life again. With a reckless fervor she threw the car around corners so fast I swore there were only two wheels on the ground half the time. I clutched her thigh and the safety holder thing above my head, praying that my seatbelt would work if it needed to. Nina grinned as madly as she drove and I knew I was going to give Tobey a piece of my mind when it was all said and done.

"Keep an eye out for a cop car." I managed to say.

"Don't worry, I'm keeping my eyes peeled."

"No, I mean I'm pretty sure they were driving a cop car."

"Oh, right," she laughed. "Crap."

I looked forward and saw an intersection ahead, and before I realized the danger Nina kicked the clutch and shifted down a gear before instantly stomping on the accelerator and pumping the handbrake, throwing the steering wheel to one side then the other, causing the car to tilt dangerously. I felt myself melt into the door, and while I was trying to hold in my lunch she was busy kicking her feet, trying to level out the throttle and the footbrake, executing a magnificent drift around the corner.

(Not that I knew what any of that was at the time.)

She had a lead foot that made the car's engine roar like a beast as it thundered down the road and I wondered why I, of all people, were in this situation right here, right now. As we drifted around another corner I saw the North Bridge that headed out the city and past the military base up ahead. Nina pushed down on the accelerator and the car bounded faster and faster.

"There!" she shouted and pointed out the windscreen. "I see a cop car, think it's them?" As I peeked ahead I felt time pause, but my grip on the car and on Nina kept them moving on through, although she had to desperately swerve to avoid a car that had stopped right in front of us.

I didn't know I could do that.

"Yeah, it's definitely them," I muttered, as they resumed time only to pause it again seconds later, forcing Nina to thread her way through a death trap of stop-starting cars. They were trying to make us crash but Nina was too good (or too bad) to let that stop her.

"So... what are we doing?" she asked, tongue stuck out as she threw the steering wheel haphazardly.

"What do you mean? We're stopping them." I watched as she zipped by a blue car at what I could only guess was mach three.

"But... how?"

"Oh right. They have guns-"

"-They have guns!?" she shrieked as time resumed. She pulled right, scraping the car against a truck but letting us narrowly escape with our lives.

"I guess we'll have to ram them?" I suggested.

"I'm not ramming them, I-"

Nina was interrupted by the car that had just stopped in front of us. She tried to escape it, but the back end of our car caught against it and though it was only a small bump, it was enough to send us spinning. I grabbed onto her thigh so hard I would be surprised if I didn't leave bruises, and she spun the steering wheel as fast as she could but it was no use. She'd lost control. Our car veered in an arc across the bridge and we crashed right into the back end of a police car and sent it spinning right as we–

Ugh... My head... It felt like church bells were ringing directly against my skull, and the feeling extended to my whole body. When I gathered enough consciousness my first instinct was to Pause. I sighed... that probably bought us some time. At least we weren't going to get rear ended and squashed like a pancake. I tried to centre my head and rearrange my thoughts, but holy crap did I ache. I guess the seat belt worked after all. My head turned like it was trapped in tar, but I needed to see if Nina was okay.

Other than some blood escaping from a cut on her forehead she seemed perfectly fine. She was unconscious, although I doubt she'd wake up as long as I had time Paused. My pain lessened, knowing she was okay. I looked out the smashed windscreen and saw bellowing smoke standing still. That can't be good, I thought as I undid my seatbelt. I fought back the airbags and had to kick my door open. It was difficult using my bad leg, but eventually the twisted metal folded and gave way enough for me to clamber out and fall onto the road. My hands scraped against the tarmac and I felt fresh cuts pour red blood, and all the dull pain sharpened to a knife point as I collided with the ground. I think my ribs were broken again, and my lip was *definitely* busted. Blood poured out from the top of my head and dripped off of my brow.

It took me forever to get back up off of the ground, but when I finally rose I could afford to look around. Cars moving at killing-speed were frozen, surrounding us on all sides, and a massive truck had been heading towards the police car. It had crashed on the opposite side of the bridge only a little further down the road. The Girl was leaning on the trunk. I couldn't see The Boy.

"Hey..." she called out weakly, pointing at a pistol sitting in the middle of the road. "Pick that up, would you?" I guessed that they'd dropped it during the crash. I limped across the road, and though bending over was absolute agony I forced myself through it and picked up the gun. I didn't know the make or the model, but it was thick, and made of black metal. It wasn't a revolver, I know that much.

I didn't like having it in my hands.

"Can you kill me please?" she asked, spitting out blood.

"This doesn't have to end in death, you know. We can talk this out." I choked on blood and coughed, covering my uniform in even more red. "You don't have to ruin the whole world to find happiness. You just have to ignore guys like Oscar and carve out a little slice for yourself."

She stepped forward and her leg buckled quite severely. Seeing that her leg was no longer able to hold her weight anymore she hopped onto the back of the car with a grunt. One of her eyes was completely drenched in scarlet, and though she wiped her sleeve across her nose it just smeared blood across her face.

"Look," I started, desperately pleading. "I can be your friend, okay? You can come to me with your problems and we can work things out!" I threw the gun as hard as I could, but she didn't care to watch as it sailed off of the bridge and into the ocean below. "Murder and killing and death aren't the only options."

The Girl smiled sadly at me.

One of the warped doors of the police car violently opened with a screech of metal on metal, and a rather long and thin leg wearing an enormous shoe came out, closely followed by another, belonging to a clown who ducked out of the car playing a horn. After him a girl somersaulted and rolled dove out of the vehicle, then came out three short dolls who walked with a stiff motion, then all the doors of all the cars on the road opened and hundreds of people dressed in a dazzling colours spilled out, bashing sticks against drums and blowing whistles so hard their faces went purple. A band playing the trumpet filtered out from the back of a miniature car, and a man on stilts riding a unicycle wheeled out from the back of a truck.

Just where the hell were these people coming from?

They all danced and sang and played a song with great cheer. But it wasn't really happy, I could tell that much despite the looks of glee I saw on their faces. We were surrounded by a crowd that was dancing and hopping and moving from one leg to the other and beating drums like there was no tomorrow and-

"I'm sorry..." The Girl said, and my gaze returned to her. Tears ran down her cheeks and mixed with her blood and dripped onto the puddle growing beneath her feet that had been spilling off the back of the car. "You don't deserve this..." she sniffled, and wiped a sleeve against her nose. "This shouldn't be your responsibility, it never should have been..."

I didn't know what to say.

"You shouldn't have to be the one to make the choice." She looked up at me, and behind her tears I saw a steely resolve. "I'll do it for you."

I felt something odd then. Something I'd never felt before. Something I didn't know could even be done. I felt a little part of me snap as she forced time to continue, despite my pause. I thought it couldn't be done.

"No, no, wait!" I screamed, reaching out to her.

The last thing I saw was a bloody, teary, heartbroken smile.
Then... The Girl was gone.

Chapter Eighteen

"It can wait until tomorrow."

I squeezed my eyes shut and tears fell out, but when I opened them again I was at the front gates to the school. There was no girl, there was no crashed police car on a bridge full of speeding death-traps, there were no cuts and scrapes on my arms, and there was no massive truck. There was just a sea of falling red leaves, a fiery floor of premature autumn.

How? Hadn't I just been on the bridge north of town? Hadn't I just watched her die!? Tobey mentioned something like this, right? Probably. I couldn't be bothered remembering anymore. I had just enough energy to stand, and even that was running out quickly. I flipped my phone open and dialled Tobey's number.

He answered on the first ring, as he always did.

"Hello?" his voice came through the speakers a little tinny.

"It's me."

"Good timing. I have just finished altering history, and wiping The Twins from existence. You did good."

"So... they're dead?"

"There's not much you could have done. This was the best possible outcome."

"Whatever," I snapped, "was none of that real?"

"Other than them dying, no, none of it was real. Oh, except for Oscar getting shot, though I'm sure you're not complaining."

I turned around and sure enough, he was there. Still writhing on the ground.

"What about... That thing with Nina?"

"I'm sorry man, that wasn't the real Nina. You never said any of that stuff to her."

"It's actually kind of a relief. Now I can take it slow."

"Oh..." he murmured in surprise. "Well be my guest then, I guess. Also I have to let you know that I don't think any of that crap."

"What crap?"

"About you being a pathetic excuse for a human."

That felt like a million years ago.

"I think you're a rather outstanding human, and a good friend."

"Thanks, I guess."

"No problem..."

Picture a man with a baseball bat.

"I'm gonna go now, but you've gotta explain this whole alien business to me soon, okay? My best friend can't be an alien without me knowing about it."

"Sure thing," he said. I could tell he was smiling, and the man put his baseball bat down. "I'll catch you later." The line went dead, but there was one more thing I needed to check.

I dialled another number.

"Where are you?" she barked. "You're missing out!"

"Nina... when's the last time you saw me?"

"Uh, the night before last. You got all screwy and weird and ran away. What was that about?"

"Don't worry about that," I said, waving my hand as if she could see it. "I was all screwy and weird, I'll be honest from now on, okay?"

"Uh, okay, sure. But where are you?"

"I'm under the oaks but I think I'm gonna go back to sleep, sorry, I need it."

She sighed. "Mind if I come over tonight?"

"Please, I'll be happy to see you."

I looked down at Oscar who was glaring at me.

"Are you... gonna call the paramedics... or what!?" he snapped.

I sighed. He did it for me, I could at least return the favour.

Epilogue

The weather was warm and the day was short, owing to the sun that shone warmly from up high, nestled within the deep blue that only a few lazy clouds tottering across. The last day of the semester had finally come, and for the whole day nobody had paid any attention to what the teachers were saying, and the teachers didn't care enough to argue. The eager chatter of friends making plans to meet up during the break filled the halls, and I took delight in the simple pleasures of friendship, smiling as I walked past.

A book flew out of the opened door to a classroom up ahead and sprawled across the floor, and though I winced as I ducked down to pick it up I was doing a lot better than a few weeks ago.

"Oh, thanks!" Lucy said, stepping out of the door with a wobble and giving me a wide smile as I placed the book on top of the stack she was precariously carrying.

"No problem. Need any help?" I asked, concerned she would topple over in a second or two.

"No need, I've got it," Akera said as she came out of the classroom behind Lucy, taking the top half of the stack from her and groaning with the sheer weight of the textbooks.

"What's with those?" I asked. Akera chuckled half-heartedly.

"It turns out that we have a *lot* to catch up on. This is all reading material for over break."

"Yeesh, sounds rough... Good luck with that."

"You can study with us sometime, if you need the catch-up," Lucy said.

"I'll consider it." I shrugged. "See you two later!" I waved goodbye as I continued my journey around the school. Luckily Akera's injuries were minor, and there was no lasting mental trauma. She had never questioned how she'd been rescued and Lucy had never brought up the topic with me again, other than one time when she had hugged me and whispered 'thank you,' with eyes full of tears.

Nina and Tobey were waiting for me by the front entrance but I'd heard from the news reporter last night that from today onwards the weather was only going to get colder, so I thought I'd better savor it. And what better way to do that than to enjoy the last day of school for as long as I could by strolling through the halls at a carefree pace? I walked past the inner courtyard where the willow tree was and sitting beneath it was David with Eileen wrapped in his arms.

"We even went to the dance together last year, and you didn't even notice I was blushing the whole time!" she laughed, looking into his eyes like he was the only thing in the world that ever mattered. David stammered, his face turning red at the touch of her hand on his cheek.

"Well... that's only 'cause I wash blushing too."

Eileen giggled, her voice piano notes chinkling, as she wrapped her arms around him and planted a kiss on his nose. "You're so cute!"

I smiled and left them to it, slightly jealous but more than happy for the couple. David and Eileen seemed like two puzzle pieces that formed a perfect picture, the kind of relationship I thought only existed in movies. Like a breeze I carried on down the halls, even taking the time to read all the posters hung up on the walls. There was one, dog-eared and aged, hanging up outside the faculty office. A reminder for the baking festival held the same day as the Athletics Celebration Day. I imagined a boy hanging it up with a scowl, then his harsh expression lighten as he saw a girl coming to say hi. I imagined them smiling. I imagined them happy.

"What is interesting?" Apronas asked as she sidled next to me. I heard a meow and looked down to see a black cat circling around her legs. I wondered if we were allowed pets on campus, but the staring eyes of the cat calculated me with such intelligence that I'm not sure that thing could be called a pet. It eked me out.

"I'm thinking of the people who hung up these posters," I answered.

Apronas looked at me. "I thought you were not so... *aismolica.*"

"I'm not, I'm *melanticos,*" I said with a wink.

She rolled her eyes, seemingly unimpressed with a few words I had learned of Urloan here and there. But I saw her smile. "Nina's looking for you. She almost talked my ear off, complaining about how long you were taking."

"So you came looking for me?"

"Do not compliment yourself so much, *Oenos.*"

I laughed. "I'll catch you later okay? Don't forget our date on the pier, Tuesday!"

"Don't call it a date!" she shouted and I laughed, finally making my way to my friends.

"What took you so long?" Nina demanded with her hands on her hips and an eyebrow raised. Shaking her head and staring at me. She looked amazing.

"Sorry, I was taking my time."

"Yeah, no joke!" she scowled and tossed my shoes at me but I just laughed through the pain. Together we walked outside, trailing behind but still a part of the crowd. Our classmates yelled and cheered, eager to escape the confines of the school grounds and start their holidays. A row of parked cars full of parents waiting for their children to hop in filled the streets. One of them was an expensive-looking black sedan with a man in a suit, opening the door for Oscar who stiffly walked over. He had caused less trouble for everyone in the last few weeks or so which I thought was surprising, considering the fact his parents had enrolled him in a different school. One far away. I thought he would take his last few opportunities to wreak havoc but he didn't. I wondered why. He stepped into the car and stopped, hesitating for a second. He turned, and took one last look at the school. Our eyes met and for a moment we stood still with locked gazes. His ice blue eyes staring at my blue sky. I gave him a nod and he returned it, then he was gone.

And life carried on, and on, and on.

I turned away and followed Nina to where Tobey was waiting for us, leaning on a telephone pole with half his shirt unbuttoned, his abs shining glorious in the evening sun.

"This again?" Nina complained.

"I'm starting to see the appeal," I joked, and Nina spun to face me with a shocked expression, causing Tobey and I to laugh at her.

"Took you long enough O-boy," Tobey said, shaking his head and buttoning up his shirt. "What were you doing?"

"I thought it was your job to know things," I snickered and he rolled his eyes.

This was probably the one day of the year I hadn't rushed out the school gates, so it wouldn't kill them to wait a few extra minutes for me to get ready. Tobey had half explained his situation about being an alien and all, but I really didn't care and just told him to zip it. He could tell me later. I think he appreciated the fact I didn't treat him any differently... Or maybe he didn't care because he was an alien robot. Who knows.

Not me.

Nina had invited everyone to her house for her birthday party tomorrow night, but Tobey and I were heading over a night early to have dinner with her and her family. Her parents were eager to see me again, and apparently her sister was looking forward to facing the legendary 'Total-Annihilation Tobey', (as he was apparently known by within certain chess circles) to a one-on-one game. We walked past the giant oak trees which were now mostly naked but still as beautiful, and together we began the journey to her home. Tobey was cracking jokes that weren't funny but we laughed anyway. With my hands in my pockets and an easy smile I looked at our comrades, all on their own way home.

Ophelia.

She was with her friends, and like us, she was laughing. This was the first time I had not felt my heart drop when I'd seen her in a long, long time. It was also the first time I had seen her happy in years. My heart didn't feel so heavy anymore.

I felt free.

Tobey walked ahead with a stiff arm and leg military man stride, and Nina shook her head as he marched away, stopping to wait for us at the peak of the next hill.

"It hasn't happened since, has it?" Nina asked, tone unhushed.

I had already explained what I could about what had happened, but I kept some things to myself. There were some skeletons still in my closet she didn't need to know about, and because Tobey asked me to keep the fact he was an alien on the down-low I had to alter some of my retelling, but Nina was fully aware about the death of the Twins. She was also aware that I hadn't been able to Pause since then.

I shook my head. "Nope. I think she broke my power, somehow."

She stepped ahead, bag clutched in her hand and almost skipping. We were on a cliff that overlooked half the city, and it was bustling far below with honking cars and eager shoppers heading to the New Business District. My gaze fell to Nina as she walked, her hair swayed over her shoulders and she was perfect. I stopped suddenly and she took a few steps to realize I was far behind, but when she did her sentence half-spoken, halted, as did her stride. She looked at me with forest-floor eyes.

"What's on your mind?" she asked.

"I'm just happy to have you as my friend." I told her. Her cheeks turned red and she looked away.

"Well... I'm happy you're my friend too," she replied, beaming a grin brighter than every star I had ever seen. Then she dug her hand into her bag and pulled out her red notebook, waving it mischievously in front of her face. "I guess we don't need this anymore," she laughed and threw her arm wide, flinging the book in an arc across the sky. Sheets of paper flew out and filled the air, and blown by the wind they whipped across the bay, taken by the sea and the Godesses.

Afterword

I have never liked afterwords. I've always thought to myself; 'I just read this bozo's book, why would I want to hear anything they have to say?', but now it's my turn and I want to be selfish. I am writing these words so that you'll read them and I'll get into your head. There is a little bit of me in you now, for better or worse. Enjoy the oncoming ramble.

I struggle with life. I agree with Oscar (and by technicality, Ophelia, who said it first). 'Life isn't like the movies, is it? There is no happy ending. The curtains don't close and the credits don't roll. It just goes on and on and on'. I feel much the same. It's almost as if I were born for a life not of this world, or I never learned how to adapt to the one I have. I've always wanted my life to have some grand meaning. I've wanted wanted to be a great hero, or to die for a righteous cause. I probably won't ever get to, but what and who I love, and what I've found meaning in, means something to me. It gives my *life* meaning. I carry pieces of the people I've loved within my soul and I am a reflection of them all, and upon my person I wear keepsakes. Rings and bracelets and buttons and broken vapes and an envelope with a 1000 yen bill inside. Life is hard, so I try to love.

Lost in Translation by Sophia Coppola is my favourite movie of all time, and it showed me that the things in life that have the most meaning are sometimes just little moments lost in time. I don't know what Bob said at the end of the movie, and I never want to. Those words were for him and Charlotte. That's how I feel about a lot of things in life. That the most important things are the times and people you bare your soul to. I am so lucky that I got to experience Japan myself, even if only for twelve days. I got lost in translation, and I found meaning again.

I know a man who believes life is all about suffering, that that's how you should live your life. That suffering great hardships is the only way to live your life. I don't agree. I've suffered enough, I should know. I think life is about living it the way you want to. You want to paint? Paint. You want to draw? Draw. Smoke? Smoke. Drink? Drink. Eat what you want, and work it off later. Bunk off work to spend a day with your wife? Be my guest. We weren't born to work, we were born to live. Some might say it's a hedonistic way to live, but I say 'screw you!' to them. 'I want to live, baby!'.

Unless you're into that, then do what you want. Why are you even listening to me?

I'm not going to live forever. Heck, I might not even live long. So I'll live as much as I can. I wanted to write, so I wrote. I want to love, so I've loved. I'll keep doing that.

Don't be like me; stuck in the past. Keep facing towards the future, there's a better day, a better love, better memories. Forget that, just live in the now. Let's all be bad children, now and forever. Onwards! I say, Ikemasho!

Really what I'm trying to say is that even if there aren't happy endings, it's the part before that where you find meaning in everything. That's the time you get to love and find friendships. I'm just some random gump. Live your life however makes you happy. Find what has meaning to you, and hold onto it.

Be careful!

Sincerely,

Theodore K. Monroe.

About the Author

Author, artist, and poet.

A man from nowhere, I crawled out of the sea one day at twenty-one years of age with no worldly knowledge but a heart full of memories from days gone by.

Printed in the USA
CPSIA information can be obtained
at www.ICGtesting.com
LVHW041511040524
779351LV00007B/190

9 798223 501985